Nora Roberts is the *New York Times* bestselling author of more than one hundred and ninety novels. A born storyteller, she creates a blend of warmth, humour and poignancy that speaks directly to her readers and has earned her almost every award for excellence in her field. The youngest of five children, Nora Roberts lives in western Maryland. She has two sons.

Visit her website at www.noraroberts.com.

Nora Roberts

Night Shield

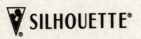
SILHOUETTE®

Silhouette and Colophon are registered trademarks of
Harlequin Books S.A., used under licence.
Silhouette Books, Eton House, 18-24 Paradise Road,
Richmond, Surrey TW9 1SR

NIGHT SHIELD © Nora Roberts 2000

ISBN: 978 0 263 87724 3

026-0210

Silhouette Books' policy is to use papers that are
natural, renewable and recyclable products and made from
wood grown in sustainable forests. The logging and
manufacturing processes conform to the legal environmental
regulations of the country of origin.

Printed and bound in Spain
by Litografia Rosés S.A., Barcelona

To tough guys, with soft hearts

Chapter 1

He didn't like cops.

His attitude had deep roots, and stemmed from spending his formative years dodging them, outrunning them—usually—or being hassled by them when his feet weren't fast enough.

He'd picked his share of pockets by the time he'd turned twelve and knew the best, and most lucrative channels for turning a hot watch into cold cash.

He'd learned back then that knowing what time

it was couldn't buy happiness, but the twenty bucks the watch brought in paid for a nice slice of the happiness pie. And twenty bucks cannily wagered swelled into sixty at three-to-one.

The same year he'd turned twelve, he'd invested his carefully hoarded takes and winnings in a small gambling enterprise that centered around point spreads and indulged his interest in sports.

He was a businessman at heart.

He hadn't run with gangs. First of all he'd never had the urge to join groups, and more importantly he didn't care for the pecking order such organizations required. Someone had to be in charge—and he preferred it to be himself.

Some people might say Jonah Blackhawk had a problem with authority.

They would be right.

He supposed the tide had turned right after he'd turned thirteen. His gambling interests had grown nicely—a little too nicely to suit certain more established syndicates.

He'd been warned off in the accepted way—he'd had the hell beat out of him. Jonah acknowledged the bruised kidneys, split lip and blackened eyes as a business risk. But before he could make his decision to move territories or dig in, he'd been busted. And busted solid.

Cops were a great deal more of an annoyance than business rivals.

But the cop who'd hauled his arrogant butt in had been different. Jonah had never pinned down what exactly separated this cop from the others in the line of shields and rule books. So, instead of being tossed into juvie—to which he was no stranger—he'd found himself yanked into programs, youth centers, counseling.

Oh, he'd squirmed and snapped in his own cold-blooded way, but this cop had a grip like a bear trap and hadn't let go. The sheer tenacity had been a shock. No one had held onto him before. Jonah had found himself rehabilitated almost despite himself, at least enough to see there were certain advantages to, if not working in the system, at least working the system.

Now, at thirty, no one would call him a pillar of Denver's community, but he was a legitimate businessman whose enterprises turned a solid profit and allowed him a lifestyle the hustling street kid couldn't have dreamed of.

He owed the cop, and he always paid his debts.

Otherwise, he'd have chosen to be chained naked and honey-smeared to a hill of fire ants rather than sit tamely in the outer office of the commissioner of police of Denver.

Even if the commissioner was Boyd Fletcher.

Jonah didn't pace. Nervous motion was wasted motion and gave too much away. The woman manning the station outside the commissioner's double doors was young, attractive with a very interesting and wanton mass of curling red hair. But he didn't flirt. It wasn't the wedding ring on her finger that stopped him as much as her proximity to Boyd, and through him, the long blue line.

He sat, patient and still, in one of the hunter-green chairs in the waiting area, a tall man with a long-legged, tough build wearing a three thousand dollar jacket over a twenty-dollar T-shirt. His hair was raven-black, rain straight and thick. That and the pale gold of his skin, the whiplash of cheekbones were gifts from his great-grandfather, an Apache.

The cool, clear green eyes might have been a legacy from his Irish great-grandmother, who'd been stolen from her family by the Apache and had given the brave who'd claimed her three sons.

Jonah knew little of his family history. His own parents had been more interested in fighting with each other over the last beer in the six-pack than tucking their only son in with bedtime stories. Occasionally Jonah's father had boasted about his lineage, but Jonah had never been sure what was fact and what was convenient fiction.

And didn't really give a damn.

You were what you made yourself.

That was a lesson Boyd Fletcher had taught him. For that alone, Jonah would have walked on hot coals for him.

"Mr. Blackhawk? The commissioner will see you now."

She offered a polite smile as she rose to get the door. And she'd taken a good, long look at the commissioner's ten o'clock appointment— a wedding ring didn't strike a woman blind, after all. Something about him made her tongue want to hang out, and at the same time made her want to run for cover.

His eyes warned a woman he'd be dangerous. He had a dangerous way of moving as well, she mused. Graceful and sleek as a cat. A woman could weave some very interesting fantasies about a man like that—and fantasies were probably the safest way to be involved with him.

Then he flicked her a smile, so full of power and charm she wanted to sigh like a teenager.

"Thanks."

She rolled her eyes as she shut the door behind him. "Oh boy, are you welcome."

"Jonah." Boyd was already up and coming around his desk. One hand gripped Jonah's while the other gave Jonah's shoulder a hard squeeze in a kind of male hug. "Thanks for coming."

"Hard to refuse a request from the commissioner."

The first time Jonah had met Boyd, Boyd had been a lieutenant. His hair had been a dark, streaked gold, and his office small, cramped and glass walled.

Now Boyd's hair was deep, solid silver, and his office spacious. The glass wall was a wide window that looked out on Denver and the mountains that ringed it.

Some things change, Jonah thought, then looked into Boyd's steady bottle-green eyes. And some don't.

"Black coffee suit you?"

"Always did."

"Have a seat." Boyd gestured to a chair then walked over to his coffee machine. He'd insisted on one of his own to save himself the annoyance of buzzing an assistant every time he wanted a hit. "Sorry I kept you waiting. I had a call to finish up. Politics," he muttered as he poured two mugs with rich black coffee. "Can't stand them."

Jonah said nothing, but the corner of his lips quirked.

"And no smart remarks about me being a damn politician at this stage of my game."

"Never crossed my mind." Jonah accepted the coffee. "To say it."

"You always were a sharp kid." Boyd sat on

a chair beside Jonah's rather than behind the desk. He let out a long sigh. "Never used to think I'd ride a desk."

"Miss the streets?"

"Every day. But you do what you do, then you do the next thing. How's the new club?"

"It's good. We draw a respectable crowd. Lots of gold cards. They need them," Jonah added as he sipped his coffee. "We hose them on the designer drinks."

"That so? And here I was thinking of bringing Cilla by for an evening out."

"You bring your wife, you get drinks and dinner on the house—is that allowed?"

Boyd hesitated, tapped his finger against his mug. "We'll see. I have a little problem, Jonah, I think you might be able to help me with."

"If I can."

"We've had a series of burglaries the last couple of months. Mostly high dollar, easily liquidated stuff. Jewelry, small electronics, cash."

"Same area?"

"No, across the board. Single family homes out in the burbs, downtown apartments, condos.

We've had six hits in just under eight weeks. Very slick, very clean."

"Well, what can I do for you?" Jonah rested his mug on his knee. "B and E was never my thing." His smile flashed. "According to my record."

"I always wondered about that." But Boyd lifted a hand, waved it away. "The marks are as varied as the locations of the hits. Young couples, older couples, singles. But they all have one thing in common. They were all at a club on the night of the burglary."

Jonah's eyes narrowed, the only change of expression. "One of mine?"

"In five out of the six, yours."

Jonah drank his coffee, looked out the wide window at the hard blue sky. The tone of his voice remained pleasant, casual. But his eyes had gone cold. "Are you asking me if I'm involved?"

"No, Jonah, I'm not asking you if you're involved. We've been beyond that for a long time." Boyd waited a beat. The boy was— always had been—touchy. "Or I have."

With a nod, Jonah rose. He walked back to the

coffeemaker, set down his cup. There weren't many people who mattered enough to him that he cared what they thought of him. Boyd mattered.

"Someone's using my place to scope marks," he said with his back to Boyd. "I don't like it."

"I didn't think you would."

"Which place?"

"The new one. Blackhawk's."

He nodded again. "Higher end clientele. Likely a bigger disposable income than the crowd at a sports bar like Fast Break." He turned back. "What do you want from me, Fletch?"

"I'd like your cooperation. And I'd like you to agree to work with the investigating team. Most specifically with the detective in charge."

Jonah swore, and in a rare show of agitation, raked his fingers through his hair. "You want me to rub shoulders with cops, set them loose in my place?"

Boyd didn't bother to hide his amusement. "Jonah, they've already been in your place."

"Not while I was there." Of that, he could be sure. He could sense cop at half a mile, while he was running in the other direction in the dark.

And had.

"No, apparently not. Some of us work during daylight hours."

"Why?"

With a half laugh, Boyd stretched out his legs. "Did I ever tell you I met Cilla when we were both on night shift?"

"No more than twenty or thirty times."

"Same smart mouth. I always liked that about you."

"That's not what you said when you threatened to staple it shut."

"Nothing wrong with your memory, either. I could use your help, Jonah." Boyd's voice went soft, serious. "I'd appreciate it."

He'd avoided prisons all his life, Jonah thought. Until Boyd. The man had built a prison around him of loyalty and trust and affection. "You've got it—for what it's worth."

"It's worth a great deal to me." He rose, offered his hand to Jonah again. "Right on time," he said as his phone rang. "Get yourself some more coffee. I want you to meet the detective in charge of the case."

He rounded the desk, picked up the receiver. "Yes, Paula. Good. We're ready." This time he sat at the desk. "I have a lot of faith in this particular cop. The detective shield's fairly new, but it was well earned."

"A rookie detective. Perfect." Resigned, Jonah poured more coffee. He didn't bobble the pot when the door opened, but his mind jumped. He supposed it was a pleasant thing to realize he could still be surprised.

She was a long-legged, lanky blonde with eyes like prime whiskey. She wore her hair in a straight, sleek tail down the middle of her back over a trim, well-cut jacket the color of steel.

When she flicked those eyes over him, her wide, pretty mouth stayed serious and unsmiling.

Jonah realized he'd have noticed the face first, so classy and fine-boned, then he'd have noticed the cop. The package might have been distracting, but he'd have made her.

"Commissioner." She had a voice like her eyes, deep and dark and potent.

"Detective. You're prompt. Jonah, this is—"

"You don't have to introduce her." Casually

Jonah sipped fresh coffee. "She has your wife's eyes and your jaw. Nice to meet you, Detective Fletcher."

"Mr. Blackhawk."

She'd seen him before. Once, she recalled, when her father had gone to one of his high school baseball games and she'd tagged along. She remembered being impressed by his gutsy, nearly violent, base running.

She also knew his history and wasn't quite as trusting of former delinquents as her father. And, though she hated to admit it, she was a little jealous of their relationship.

"Do you want some coffee, Ally?"

"No, sir." He was her father, but she didn't sit until the commissioner gestured to a chair.

Boyd spread his hands. "I thought we'd be more comfortable having this meeting here. Ally, Jonah's agreed to cooperate with the investigation. I've given him the overview. I leave it to you to fill in the necessary details."

"Six burglaries in a period of under eight weeks. Estimated cumulative loss in the ballpark of eight hundred thousand dollars. They go for easily fenced items, heavy on the jewelry. However, in one case a victim's Porsche was stolen from the garage. Three of the homes had security systems. They were disengaged. There have been no signs of break-in. In each case the residence was empty at the time of the burglary."

Jonah crossed the room, sat. "I've already got that much—except for the Porsche. So, you've got someone who can boost cars as well as lift locks, and likely has a channel to turn over a variety of merchandise."

"None of the goods have turned up through any of the known channels in Denver. The operation's well organized and efficient. We suspect there are at least two, probably three or more people involved. Your club's been the main source."

"And?"

"Two of your employees at Blackhawk's have criminal records. William Sloan and Frances Cummings."

Jonah's eyes went cold, but didn't flicker. "Will ran numbers, and did his time. He's been out and clean for five years. Frannie worked the stroll, and it's her business why. Now she tends bar instead of johns. Don't you believe in rehabilitation, Detective Fletcher?"

"I believe your club is being used as a pool to hook fish, and I intend to check all the lines. Logic indicates someone on the inside's baiting the hook."

"I know the people who work for me." He shot Boyd a furious look. "Damn it, Fletch."

"Jonah, hear us out."

"I don't want my people hassled because they tripped over the law at some point in their lives."

"No one's going to hassle your people. Or you," Ally added. Though you did plenty of tripping of your own, she thought. "If we'd wanted to interview them, we would have. We don't need your permission or your cooperation to question potential suspects."

"You move them from my people to suspects very smoothly."

"If you believe they're innocent, why worry?"

"Okay, simmer down." Boyd stayed behind the desk, rubbed the back of his neck. "You're in an awkward and difficult position, Jonah. We appreciate that," he said pointedly with a subtle lift of his eyebrows for his daughter. "The goal is to root out whoever's in charge of this organization and put an end to it. They're using you."

"I don't want Will and Frannie yanked down into interrogation."

"That's not our intention." So he had a hot button, Ally mused. Friendship? Loyalty? Or maybe he had a thing going with the ex-hooker. It would be part of the job to find out. "We don't want to alert anyone on the inside to the investigation. We need to find out who's targeting the marks, and how. We want you to put a cop on the inside."

"I'm on the inside," he reminded her.

"Then you should be able to make room for another waitress. I can start tonight."

Jonah let out a short laugh, turned to Boyd. "You want your daughter working tables in my club?"

Ally got to her feet, slowly. "The commissioner wants one of his detectives undercover at your club. And this is my case."

Jonah rose as well. "Let's clear this up. I don't

give a damn whose case it is. Your father asked me to cooperate, so I will. Is this what you want me to do?" he asked Boyd.

"It is, for now."

"Fine. She can start tonight. Five o'clock, my office at Blackhawk's. We'll go over what you need to know."

"I owe you for this, Jonah."

"You'll never owe me for anything." He walked to the door, stopped, shot a glance over his shoulder. "Oh, Detective? Waitresses at Blackhawk's wear black. Black shirt or sweater, black skirt. Short black skirt," he added, then let himself out.

Ally pursed her lips, and for the first time since she'd come into the room relaxed enough to slip her hands casually into her pockets. "I don't think I like your friend, Dad."

"He'll grow on you."

"What, like mold? No," she corrected. "He's too cool for that. I might end up with a little skin of ice, though. You're sure of him?"

"As sure as I am of you."

And that, she thought, said it all. "Whoever's

set up these B and E's has brains, connections and guts. I'd say your pal there has all three." She lifted her shoulders. "Still, if I can't trust your judgment, whose can I trust?"

Boyd grinned. "Your mother always liked him."

"Well then, I'm half in love already." That wiped the grin off his face, she noted with amusement. "I'm still going to have a couple of men under as customers."

"That's your call."

"It's been five days since the last hit. They're working too well not to want to move again soon."

She strode toward the coffeepot, changed her mind and strode away again. "They might not use his club next time, it's not a given. We can't cover every damn club in the city."

"So, you focus your energy on Blackhawk. That's smart, and it's logical. One step at a time, Allison."

"I know. I learned that from the best. I guess the first step is to go dig up a short black skirt."

Boyd winced as she walked to the door. "Not too short."

* * *

Ally had the eight-to-four shift at the precinct, and even if she left on the dot and sprinted the four blocks from the station to her apartment, she couldn't get home before 4:10.

She knew. She'd timed it.

And leaving at exactly four was as rare as finding diamonds in the mud. But damned if she wanted to be late for her next meeting with Blackhawk.

It was a matter of pride and principle.

She slammed into her apartment at 4:11—thanks to the delay of a last-minute briefing by her lieutenant—and peeled off her jacket as she raced to the bedroom.

Blackhawk's was a good twenty minutes away at a brisk jog—and half again that much if she attempted to drive in rush hour traffic.

It was only her second undercover assignment behind her detective's shield. She had no intention of screwing it up.

She released her shoulder harness and tossed it onto the bed. Her apartment was simple and uncluttered, mostly because she wasn't there long enough for it to be otherwise. The house where she'd grown up was still home, the station house was second on that list of priorities, and the apartment where she slept, occasionally ate and even more rarely loitered, was a far down third.

She'd always wanted to be a cop. She hadn't made a big deal of it. It simply was her dream.

She yanked open her closet door and pushed through a selection of clothes—designer dresses, tailored jackets and basketball jerseys— in search of a suitable black skirt.

If she could manage a quick change, she might actually have time to slap together a sandwich or stuff a handful of cookies into her mouth before she raced out again.

She pulled out a skirt, winced at the length when she held it up, then tossed that on the bed as well to dig through her dresser for a pair of black hose.

If she was going to wear a skirt that barely covered her butt, she would damn well cover the rest with solid, opaque black.

Tonight could be the night, she thought as she stripped off her trousers. She had to stay calm about it, cool, controlled.

She would use Jonah Blackhawk, but she would not be distracted by him.

She knew a great deal about him through her father, and she'd made it her business to find out more. As a kid he'd had light fingers, quick feet and a nimble brain. She could almost admire a boy with barely twelve years under his belt who'd managed to organize a sports' betting syndicate. Almost.

And she supposed she could come close to admiring someone who'd turned those beginnings around—at least on the surface—and made himself into a successful businessman.

The fact was she'd been in his sports' bar and had enjoyed the atmosphere, the service and the truly superior margaritas Fast Break provided.

The place had a terrific selection of pinball machines, she recalled. Unless someone had broken her record in the last six months, her initials were still in the number one slot on Double Play.

She really should make time to get back there and defend her championship status.

But that was beside the point, she reminded

herself. Right now the point was Jonah Blackhawk.

Maybe his feathers were ruffled because she'd made it clear that two of his employees were on her short list of suspects. Well, that was too bad. Her father wanted her to trust the man, so she'd do her best to trust him.

As far as she could throw him.

By 4:20, she was dressed in black—turtleneck, skirt, hose. She shoved through the shoes on the floor of her closet and found a suitable pair of low heels.

With a nod to vanity, she dragged the clip out of her hair, brushed it, clipped it back again. Then she closed her eyes and tried to think like a waitress in an upscale club.

Lipstick, perfume, earrings. An attractive waitress made more tips, and tips had to be a goal. She took the time for them, then studied the results in the mirror.

Sexy, she supposed, certainly feminine and in a satisfactory way, practical. And there was no place to hide her weapon.

Damn it. She hissed out a breath, and settled

on stuffing her nine millimeter in an oversize shoulder bag. She tossed on a black leather jacket as a concession to the brisk spring evening, then bolted for the door.

There was enough time to drive to the club if she got straight down to the garage and hit all the lights on green.

She pulled open the door. Swore.

"Dennis, what are you doing?"

Dennis Overton held up a bottle of California Chardonnay and offered a big, cheerful smile. "Just in the neighborhood. Thought we could have a drink."

"I'm on my way out."

"Fine." He shifted the bottle, tried to take her hand. "I'll go with you."

"Dennis." She didn't want to hurt him. Not again. He'd been so devastated when she'd broken things off two months before. And all his phone calls, pop-ins, run-intos since then had ended badly. "We've been through all this."

"Come on, Ally. Just a couple of hours. I miss you."

He had that sad, basset hound look in his eyes,

that pleading smile on his lips. It had worked once, she reminded herself. More than once. But she remembered how those same eyes could blaze with wild and misplaced jealousy, snap with barely controlled fury.

She'd cared for him once, enough to forgive him his accusations, to try to work through his mood swings, enough to feel guilty over ending it.

She cared enough now to strap her temper at this last invasion of her time and her space. "I'm sorry, Dennis. I'm in a hurry."

Still smiling, he blocked her way. "Give me five minutes. One drink for old times' sake, Ally?"

"I don't have five minutes."

The smile vanished, and that old, dark gleam leaped into his eyes. "You never had time for me when I needed it. It was always what you wanted and when you wanted it."

"That's right. You're well rid of me."

"You're going to see someone else, aren't you? Brushing me off so you can run off to be with another man."

"What if I am." Enough, she thought, was way past enough. "It's no business of yours where I go, what I do, whom I see. That's what you can't seem to get straight. But you're going to have to work harder at it, Dennis, because I'm sick of this. Stop coming here."

He grabbed her arm before she could walk by. "I want to talk to you."

She didn't jerk free, only stared down at his hand, then shifted her gaze, icy as February, to his eyes. "Don't push it. Now step back."

"What're you going to do? Shoot me? Arrest me? Call your daddy, the saint of the police, to lock me up?"

"I'm going to ask you, one more time, to step back. Step way back, Dennis, and do it now."

His mood swung again, fast and smooth as a revolving door. "I'm sorry. Ally, I'm sorry." His eyes went damp and his mouth trembled. "I'm upset, that's all. Just give me another chance. I just need another chance. I'll make it work this time."

She pried his fingers off her arm. "It never worked. Go home, Dennis. I've got nothing for you."

She walked away without looking back, bleeding inside because she had to. Bleeding inside because she could.

Chapter 2

Ally hit the doors of Blackhawk at 5:05. One strike against her, she thought and took an extra minute to smooth down her hair, catch her breath. She'd decided against the drive after all and had run the ten blocks. Not such a distance, she thought, but the heels she wore were a far cry from track shoes.

She stepped inside, took stock.

The bar was a long, gleaming black slab that curved into a snug semicircle and offered plenty of room for a troop of chrome stools with thick, black leather cushions. Mirrored panels of black and silver ran down the rear wall, tossed back reflections and shapes.

Comfort, she decided, as well as style. It said, sit down, relax and plunk down your money.

There were plenty of people to do so. Apparently happy hour was underway, and every stool was occupied. Those who sat at the bar, or kicked back at the chrome tables, drank and nibbled to the tune of recorded music kept low enough to encourage conversation.

Most of the patrons were the suit-and-tie crowd with briefcases dumped at their feet. The business brigade, she concluded, who'd managed to slip out of the office a little early, or were using the club as a meeting arena to discuss deals or close them.

Two waitresses worked the tables. Both wore black, but she noted with a hiss through her teeth that they wore slacks rather than skirts.

A man was working the bar—young, handsome and openly flirting with the trio of women on stools at the far end. She wondered when

Frances Cummings came on shift. She'd need to get work schedules from Blackhawk.

"You look a little lost."

Ally shifted her gaze and studied the man who approached her with an easy smile. Brown hair, brown eyes, trim beard. Five-ten, maybe one-fifty. His dark suit was well cut, his gray tie neatly knotted.

William Sloan looked a great deal more presentable tonight than he had for his last mug shot.

"I hope not." Deciding a little agitation fit the role, Ally shifted her shoulder bag and offered a nervous smile. "I'm Allison. I'm supposed to see Mr. Blackhawk at five. I guess I'm late."

"Couple of minutes. Don't worry about it. Will Sloan." He offered a hand, gave hers a quick, brotherly squeeze. "The man told me to keep an eye out for you. I'll take you up."

"Thanks. Great place," she commented.

"You bet. The man's in charge, and he wants the best. I'll give you a quick go-through." With a hand on her back, Will led her through the bar area, into a wide room with more tables, a two-level stage and a dance floor.

Silver ceilings, she mused, glancing up, set with pinpoint lights that blinked and shimmered. The tables were black squares on pedestals that rose out of a smoky silver floor with those same little lights twinkling under the surface, like stars behind clouds.

The art was modern, towering canvases splashed or streaked with wild colors, odd, intriguing wall sculptures fashioned from metals or textiles.

The tables were bare but for a slim metal cylindrical lamp with cut-outs in the shape of crescent moons.

Deco meets the third millennium, she decided. Jonah Blackhawk had built himself a very classy joint.

"You work clubs before?"

She'd already decided how to play it and rolled her eyes. "Nothing like this. Pretty fancy."

"The man wanted class. The man gets class." He turned down a corridor, then punched a code into a control panel. "Watch this."

When a panel in the wall slid open, he wiggled his eyebrows. "Cool, huh?"

"Major." She stepped in with him, watched him reenter the code.

"Any of us who've got to do business on the second level get a code. You won't have to worry about it. So, you new in Denver?"

"No, actually I grew up here."

"No bull? Me, too. I've been hanging with the man since we were kids. Life sure was different then."

The door opened again, directly into Jonah's office. It was a large space, split into business and pleasure with an area to one side devoted to a long leather sofa in his signature color, two sink-into-me armchairs and a wide-screen TV where a night baseball game was being battled out in silence.

Automatically she checked the stats in the top corner of the screen. Yankees at home against Toronto. Bottom of the first. Two out, one on. No score.

The focus on sports didn't surprise her, but the floor-to-ceiling shelves of books did.

She shifted her attention to the business area. It appeared to be as ruthlessly efficient as the rest of the room was indulgent. The workstation held a computer and phone. Across from it stood a monitor that showed the club area. The single window was shielded with blinds, and the blinds were tightly shut. The carpet was cozily thick and stone-gray.

Jonah sat at the desk, his back to the wall, and held up a hand as he completed a call. "I'll get back to you on that. No, not before tomorrow." He lifted a brow as if amused by what was said to him. "You'll just have to wait."

He hung up, sat back in his chair. "Hello, Allison. Thanks, Will."

"No problem. Catch you later, Allison."

"Thanks a lot."

Jonah waited until the elevator door shut. "You're late."

"I know. It was unavoidable." She turned to the monitor giving him an opportunity to skim his gaze down her back, over those long legs.

Very nice, he thought. Very nice indeed.

"You have security cameras throughout the public areas?"

"I like to know what's going on in my place."

She just bet he did. "Do you keep the tapes?"

"We turn them over every three days."

"I'd like to see what you've got." Because her back was to him, she allowed her gaze to slide over and check the action in Yankee Stadium. Toronto brought one home on a line drive bullet. "It'll help to study the tapes."

"For that you'll need a warrant."

She glanced back over her shoulder. He'd changed into a suit—black and to her expert eye, of Italian cut. "I thought you'd agreed to cooperate."

"To a point. You're here, aren't you?" His phone rang and was ignored. "Why don't you sit down? We'll work out a game plan."

"The game plan's simple." And she didn't sit. "I pose as a waitress, talk to customers and staff. I keep my eyes open and do my job. You keep out of my way and do yours."

"Wrong plan. I don't have to keep out of anyone's way in my place. Now, ever worked a club?"

"No."

"Ever waited tables?"

"No." His cool, patient look irked. "What's the big deal. You take the order, you put in the order, you serve the order. I'm not a moron."

He smiled now, that quick, powerful strike. "I imagine it seems that way when you've spent your life on the other side of it. You're about to get an education, Detective. Head waitress on your shift is Beth. She'll help train you. Until you've got a handle on it, you'll bus tables. That means—"

"I know what busing tables involves."

"Fine, I've put you on six to two. You get a fifteen minute break every two hours. No drinking during shift. Any of the customers get overly friendly or out of line, you report to me or to Will."

"I can handle myself."

"You're not a cop here. Somebody puts hands on you in an inappropriate way, you report to me or to Will."

"You get a lot of that?"

"Only from the women. They can't keep their hands off me."

"Ha-ha."

Out of the corner of his eye, he noted the

Yankees ended the inning on a strikeout. "No, we don't get a lot of it, but it happens. Some guys cross lines when they drink. They only cross them in my place once. The crowd starts getting thick after eight. Entertainment starts at nine. You'll be busy."

He got to his feet, walked to her, walked around her. "You've got a nice cover over the cop in you. You have to look hard to see it. I like the skirt."

She waited until he'd come around and they were face-to-face. "I'll need work schedules for all employees. Or do I need a warrant?"

"No, I can help you out there." He liked the scent of her. Cool and clearly female. "I'll have printouts for you by closing. Anyone I hire who I don't know personally—and even some I do—goes through a full background check. Not everyone here's been lucky enough to come from a nice, tidy family and live a nice, tidy life."

Jonah picked up a remote, switched the angle of the cameras so the bar area popped on screen. "Kid just coming off shift at the bar? Grew up with his grandparents when his mother ran off. Got into a little trouble when he was fifteen."

"And what kind of trouble was that?"

"Got tagged with a joint in his pocket. He straightened out, they sealed the records, but he was up-front with me when he wanted the job. He's putting himself through night school."

At the moment she wasn't interested in the young man going off shift at the bar. She kept her eyes on Jonah. "Is everyone up-front with you?"

"The smart one's are. That's Beth." He tapped the screen.

Ally saw a little brunette, about thirty, come in through a door behind the bar.

"Bastard she was married to used to kick her around. She can't weigh a hundred pounds. She's got three kids at home. Sixteen, twelve and ten. She's been working for me on and off about five years, used to come in every couple weeks with a black eye or split lip. She took the kids and left him two years ago."

"Is he leaving her alone?"

Jonah shifted his gaze to Ally's. "He was persuaded to relocate."

"I see." And she did. Jonah Blackhawk looked after his own. She couldn't fault him for it. "Did he relocate in one piece?"

"Mostly. I'll take you down. You can leave your bag up here if you want."

"No, thanks."

He pushed the button for the elevator. "I assume you've got your gun in there. Keep it in there. There's a secure employee area off the bar. You can lock it up in there. This shift Beth and Frannie have keys. Will and I have keys or codes for all areas at all times."

"Tight ship, Blackhawk."

"That's right. What's the cover?" he asked as they stepped into the elevator. "How'd I meet you?"

"I needed a job, you gave me a job." She shrugged. "Keep it simple. I caught you at your sports bar."

"Know anything about sports?"

She sent him a smile. "Anything that takes place off a field, a court or outside an arena is just marking time."

"Where have you been all my life?" He took

her arm as they stepped out on the main floor. "So, Jays or Yankees?"

"Yankees have stronger bats this season and rule the long ball, but their gloves are sloppy. The Jays chip away with reliable base hits, and their infield's a ballet of guts and efficiency. I go for guts and efficiency over the power stroke every time."

"Is that a baseball statement, or a life statement?"

"Blackhawk, baseball is life."

"Now you've done it. We have to get married."

"My heart's all aflutter," she said dryly and turned to scan the bar area. The noise level had bumped up several notches. They were two and three deep at the curved black slab now, the after work, before dinner crowd.

For some it was unwind time, she thought, for others a casual mating ritual. But for someone, it was a hunt.

People were so careless, she mused. She saw men leaning on the bar, back pockets ripe for picking. More than one handbag hung vulnerable on the back of a stool or chair. Coats and jackets, some likely to have car or house keys in their pockets, were tossed aside.

"Nobody ever thinks it can happen to them," Ally murmured, then tapped Jonah's arm, inclined her head. "Check out the guy at the bar— six down, with the news-anchor hair and teeth."

Amused, Jonah tagged the guy from Ally's description and watched him flash his wallet, choked with bills and credit cards.

"He's trying to lure the redhead there, or her pretty blond friend. Doesn't matter which. Odds are he hits with the blonde," Jonah concluded.

"Why?"

"Call it a hunch." He looked down at Ally. "Wanna bet?"

"You don't have a license for gambling on the premises." As she watched, the blonde sidled over and batted her lashes at the man with the wallet. "Good call."

"It was easy. And so's the blonde." He steered Ally back toward the club area where Beth and Will huddled over the reservation book at a black podium.

"Hey, boss." Beth plucked the pencil out of

her thick curls and made a note in the book. "Looks like we're turning most tables over twice tonight. Big dinner crowd for midweek."

"Good thing I brought you some help. Beth Dickerman, Allison Fletcher. She needs training."

"Ah, another victim." Beth shot out a hand. "Nice to meet you, Allison."

"Ally. Thanks."

"You show her the ropes, Beth. She'll bus tables until you figure she can wait them."

"We'll whip her into shape. Come on with me, Ally. I'll get you set up. Got any experience in food services?" she asked as she plowed through the crowd.

"Well, I eat."

Beth let out a bright cackle of a laugh. "Welcome to my world. Frannie, this is Ally, new waitress in training. Frannie's captain of the bar here."

"Nice to meetcha," Frannie called out, flipped a smile, dumping ice into a blender with one hand and shooting soda into a glass with the other.

"And that gorgeous specimen down the other end of the bar's Pete."

The big shouldered black man sent them a wink as he measured Kahlua into a short glass.

"Now, no flirting with Pete, 'cause he's my man and nobody else's. That right, Pete?"

"You're the one for me, sugar lips."

With another laugh, Beth unlocked a door marked Employees Only. "Pete's got a beautiful wife and a baby on the way. We just tease. Now, if you need to get in here for any reason— hey, Jan."

"Hey, Beth." The curvy brunette on the other side of the door had her waist-length hair pulled back with combs from a lovely, heart-shaped face. Ally gauged her as mid-twenties, and a fashion plate. She'd gone for a skirt the approximate size of a table napkin, and a clingy shirt with small silver buttons. Silver winked at her wrists, ears and throat as she freshened her lipstick in a mirror.

"This is Ally. Fresh meat."

"Oh, yeah." The smile when she turned was friendly enough, but there was a measuring gleam in her eye. One female sizing up another, and the competition.

"Jan works the bar area," Beth explained. "But she'll pinch hit in the club if we need her." There was a wild burst of laughter from outside the door. "Tom-toms are beating."

"I'd better get out there." Jan tied a short, many-pocketed black apron at her waist. "Good luck, Ally, and welcome aboard."

"Thanks. Everybody's so friendly," Ally said to Beth when Jan strolled out.

"You get to be kind of a family when you work for Jonah. He's a good boss." She pulled an apron out of a closet. "You work your butt off for him, but he lets you know he notices and that he appreciates. Makes a difference. Here, you'll need this."

"Have you worked for him long?"

"About six years, give or take. I handled tables at Fast Break, his sports bar. And when he opened the club here, he asked me if I wanted to switch. It's a classy place, and closer to home. You can leave your purse in here." She opened a narrow locker. "You reset the combination by spinning around zero twice."

"Great." Ally set her purse inside, palming her beeper out of it and hooking it on the waist of her skirt under the apron. She shut the locker, set the combination. "I guess that's it."

"You want to freshen up or anything?"

"No, I'm fine. A little nervous, I guess."

"Don't worry. In a few hours your feet are going to ache so bad you won't think about nerves."

Beth was right. About the feet anyway. By ten, Ally felt she'd hiked twenty miles in the wrong shoes, and lifted approximately three tons of trays loaded with dirty dishes.

She could have marched the trail from table to kitchen in her sleep.

The live band was considerably louder than the recorded music that had played until just after nine. The crowd shouted above it, crammed the dance floor and jammed together at the tables.

Ally piled dishes on trays and watched the crowd. There were plenty of designer clothes, expensive watches, cell phones and leather brief-cases. She saw a woman flash a lightning bolt diamond engagement ring for three friends.

Plenty of money here, she noted. And plenty of marks.

Hefting the loaded tray, she headed off for the kitchen, detouring toward an attractive couple when the man signaled her.

"Sweetheart, can you get me and my lovely companion a refill here?"

She leaned closer, pasted on her sweetest smile and made a quiet and crude suggestion.

The man only grinned. "Cops have such filthy mouths."

"Next case I'm going to be the one sitting on my butt, Hickman, while you work out," Ally replied. "See anything I should know about?"

"Nothing's popped yet." He grabbed the hand of the woman sitting next to him. "But Carson and I are in love."

Lydia Carson gave Hickman's hand a vicious squeeze. "In your dreams."

"Just keep your eyes open." She aimed a stare at Hickman's glass. "And that'd better be club soda."

"She's so strict," she heard Hickman murmur as she walked away.

"Beth, table…ah, sixteen's looking for a refill."

"I'm on it. You're doing good, Ally. Go dump those and take your break."

"You don't have to tell me twice."

The kitchen was a madhouse, full of noise and shouted orders and heat. Gratefully Ally set down her tray, then lifted her eyebrows as she spotted Frannie slipping out the back door.

Ally stalled for ten seconds, then followed.

Frannie was already leaning against the outside wall and taking her first drag from a cigarette. She blew out smoke with a long, relieved sigh. "Break time?"

"Yeah. I thought I'd grab some air."

"Zoo in there tonight. Blackhawk's really packs them in." She pulled the cigarettes out of her pocket, offered them.

"No, thanks. I don't smoke."

"Good for you. I can't kick it. No smoking in the employee lounge. Jonah gives me a break and lets me use his office if the weather's lousy. So how's your first night?"

"My feet are killing me."

"Occupational hazard. First paycheck you buy yourself one of those bubbling footbath things. Put some eucalyptus in it, and go straight to heaven."

"I'll do that."

An attractive woman, Ally noted, though the lines around Frannie's eyes made her look older than twenty-eight. She kept her dark red hair cut short and the makeup subtle. Her nails were short and unpainted, her hands ringless. Like the rest of the staff, she wore black, and finished off the simple shirt and slacks with sturdy yet trendy black shoes.

The only touch of flash was the silver hoops that swung at her ears.

"How'd you get into tending bar?" Ally asked her.

Frannie hesitated, then puffed on her cigarette. "I guess I hung out at bars a lot, and when there came a time I was looking for what you could call gainful employment, Jonah asked me if I wanted a job. Trained me over at Fast Break. It's good work. You need a decent memory and people skills. You interested?"

"I'd better see if I make it through one shift busing before I start raising my sights."

"You look like you can handle whatever comes along."

Ally smiled into Frannie's considering eyes. "You think so?"

"Observation's one of those people skills. And on short observation you don't strike me as the type who expects to make waiting tables her life's work."

"Gotta start somewhere. And paying the rent's a priority."

"Don't I know it." Though Frannie had already calculated that Ally's shoes equaled half a month's rent on her own apartment. "Well, if you want to climb the ladder, Jonah's the one to give you a boost. You'd have figured that."

Frannie dropped the cigarette, crushed out the butt. "Gotta get back. Pete pouts if I go over break."

The ex-hooker, Ally decided, was proprietary when it came to Jonah. They were probably lovers, she thought as she went back inside. When you factored in his defensive attitude toward her, it added up.

As lover, as trusted employee, Frannie was in

a prime position to cull out marks, to pass the information along. The bar faced the entrance. Whoever went in or out passed by her station.

People handed her credit cards, and the name and account number led to addresses.

It would pay to look at her most closely.

Jonah was doing his own looking. From his office, from the floor. He knew enough about cons, short and long, to calculate who the targets might be. He pegged three possibilities that would have topped his list if he'd been running the game. And since he'd also spotted the cops at table sixteen, he wandered over.

"Everything all right tonight?"

The woman beamed up at him, swept back her short swing of streaky blond hair with one hand. "Everything's terrific. It's the first night on the town Bob and I have managed in weeks with work keeping both of us so busy."

"I'm glad you picked my place." Jonah laid a friendly hand on Bob's shoulder, leaned down. "Next time ditch the cop shoes. Dead giveaway. Enjoy your evening."

He thought he heard the woman snort out a laugh as he walked away.

He headed for the table Ally was busy cleaning. "How you holding up?"

"I haven't broken any of your dishes yet."

"And now you want a raise?"

"I'm going to stick with my day job, thanks all the same. I'd rather clean up the streets than tables." Absently she pressed a hand to the ache in the small of her back.

"We go back to bar food at eleven, so the busing slows down."

"Hallelujah."

He laid a hand on her arm before she could lift the tray. "You corner Frannie outside?"

"Excuse me?"

"She went out, you went out, she came in, you came in."

"I'm doing my job. However, I resisted shining a light in her eyes and smacking her in the face with my rubber hose. Now let me get on with it."

She hefted the tray, shoved past him.

"By the way, Allison."

She stopped, a snarl working up her throat. "What?"

"The power ball trounced your guts and efficiency. Eight to two."

"One game doesn't a season make." She jerked up her chin and strode off. On her way by the dance floor, a man reached out and gave her butt a hopeful pat. As Jonah watched she stopped dead in her tracks, turned slowly and gave him one, long icy look. The man stepped back, lifted his hands in apology and quickly melted into the dancers.

"Handles herself," Beth said from beside him.

"Yeah. Yeah, she does."

"Pulls her weight, too, and doesn't whine about it. I like your girlfriend, Jonah."

He was too surprised to comment and only stared when Beth hustled away.

He let out a short laugh and shook his head. Oh, that one had slipped by him. Right on by him.

Last call was enough to make Ally all but weep with gratitude. She'd been on her feet since eight that morning. Her fondest wish was to go home, fall into bed and sleep for the precious five hours she had before starting it all over again.

"Go on home," Beth ordered. "We'll go over closing tomorrow night. You did fine."

"Thanks. I mean it."

"Will, let Ally into the lounge, will you?"

"No problem. Nice crowd tonight. Nothing I like better than a crowded club. Want a drink before you head out?"

"Not unless I can stick my feet in it."

He chuckled, patted her back. "Frannie, pour me one, will you?"

"Already on it."

"I like a brandy at the end of a shift. One glass of the good stuff. You change your mind," he said as he unlocked the door. "Just pull up a stool. The man, he doesn't charge employees for an end of shift drink."

He went off, whistling through his teeth.

Ally shoved her apron into her locker, pulled out her bag and jacket. She was just putting the jacket on when Jan breezed in. "Heading out? You look beat. Me, I'm just hitting stride this time of night."

"My stride hit me about an hour ago." Ally paused at the door. "Don't your feet hurt?"

"Nah. I got arches of steel. And most guys tip better if you walk around on skinny heels." She bent to run a hand up her leg. "I believe in using what works."

"Yeah. Well, good night."

Ally stepped out of the lounge, shutting the door behind her, and bumped solidly into Jonah.

"Where'd you park?" he asked her.

"I didn't. I walked." Ran, she remembered, but it came to the same thing.

"I'll drive you home."

"I can walk. It's not far."

"It's two in the morning. A block is too far."

"For heaven's sake, Blackhawk, I'm a cop."

"So naturally, bullets bounce off you."

Before she could argue, he caught her chin in his hand. The gesture, the firm grip of his fingers, shocked her to silence. "You're not a cop at the moment," he murmured. "You're a female employee and the daughter of a friend. I'll drive you home."

"Fine. Dandy. My feet hurt anyway."

She started to shove his hand away, but he beat her to it and shifted his grip to her arm.

"Night, boss." Beth called out, grinning at them as they passed. "Get that girl off her feet."

"That's my plan. Later, Will. Night, Frannie."

Suspicion was buzzing in Ally's brain as Will lifted his brandy snifter and Frannie watched her with quiet and serious eyes.

"What was that?" Ally demanded when they stepped out in the cool air. "What exactly was that?"

"That was me saying good-night to friends and employees. I'm parked across the street."

"Excuse me, my feet have gone numb, not my brain. You gave those people the very distinct impression that we have a thing here."

"That's right. I didn't consider it, either, until Beth made some remark earlier. It simplifies things."

She stopped beside a sleek black Jaguar. "Just how do you figure that having people think there's a personal thing between us simplifies anything?"

"And you call yourself a detective." He

unlocked the passenger door, opened it. "You're a beautiful blonde with legs up to your ears. I hire you, out of the blue, when you have basically no experience. The first assumption from people who know me is I'm attracted to you. The second would be you're attracted to me. Add all those together and you end up with romance. Or at least sex. Are you going to get in?"

"You haven't explained how those deductions equal simple."

"If people think we're involved they won't think twice if I give you a little leeway, if you come up to my office. They'll be friendlier."

Ally said nothing while she let it run through her head. Then she nodded. "All right. There's an advantage to it."

Going with impulse he shifted, boxed her in between his body and the car door. There was a light breeze, just enough to stir her scent. There was a three-quarter moon, bright enough to sprinkle silver into her eyes. The moment, he decided, seemed to call for it.

"Could be more than one advantage to it."

The thrill that sprinted straight up her spine

irritated her. "Oh, you're going to want to step back, Blackhawk."

"Beth's at the window of the bar, and she's got a romantic heart despite everything that's happened to her. She's hoping for a moment here. A long, slow kiss, the kind that slides over melting sighs and heats the blood."

His hands came to her hips as he spoke, rode up to just under her breasts. Her mouth went dry and the ache in her belly was a wide stretch of longing.

"You're going to have to disappoint her."

Jonah skimmed his gaze down to her mouth. "She's not the only one." But he released her, stepped back. "Don't worry, Detective. I never hit on cops, or daughters of friends."

"Then I guess I've got a double shield against your wild and irresistible charms."

"Good thing for both of us, because I sure as hell like the look of you. You getting in?"

"Yeah, I'm getting in." She got into the car and waited until the door shut before letting out the long, painful breath she'd been holding.

Wherever that spurt of lust inside her had come from, it would just have to go away again.

Cool off, she ordered herself, but her heart was bumping madly against her rib cage. Cool off and focus on the job.

Jonah slid in beside her, annoyed that his pulse wasn't quite steady. "Where to?" When she rattled off the address, he shoved the key into the ignition and aimed one hot look at her. "That's a damn mile. Why the hell did you walk?"

"Because it was rush hour. It's quicker. And it's ten blocks."

"That's just stupid."

She had a response for that. The venom of it scalded her tongue as she rounded on him. She didn't even recognize the vibration of her beeper for several seconds, mistaking it for the vibration of rage.

She yanked it from her skirt, checked the number. "Damn it. Damn it." From her purse she pulled out her cell phone and quickly dialed. "Detective Fletcher. Yeah, I got it. I'm on my way."

Calming herself, she shoved the phone back into her purse. "Since you're determined to play cab driver, let's get going. I've got another B and E."

"Give me the address."

"Just take me home so I can get my car."

"Give me the address, Allison. Why waste time?"

Chapter 3

Jonah dropped her off in front of an attractive, ranch-style home in an upscale development convenient to the freeway. In reasonable traffic, the commute to downtown would take under twenty minutes.

The Chamberses, Ally discovered, were an attractive, upscale couple, both lawyers in their early thirties, childless professionals, who spent their comfortable income on the good life.

Wine, wardrobe, jewelry, art and music.

"They got my diamond earrings, and my Cartier tank watch." Maggie Chambers rubbed her eyes as she sat in what was left of her sprawling great room. "We haven't gone through everything, but there were Dalí and Picasso lithographs on that wall there. And in that niche there was an Erté sculpture we bought at an auction two years ago. Joe collected cuff links. I don't know how many pairs he had offhand, but he had diamond ones, and ruby for his birthstone and several antique pairs."

"They're insured." Her husband reached out to take her hand, squeeze it.

"It doesn't matter. It's not the same. Those thugs were in our house. In our house, Joe, and they've taken our things. Damn it, they stole my car. My brand-new BMW, and it didn't have five thousand miles on it. I loved that stupid car."

"Mrs. Chambers, I know it's hard."

Maggie Chambers whipped her gaze toward Ally. "Have you ever been robbed, Detective?"

"No." Ally set her notebook on her knee a moment. "But I've worked plenty of burglaries, robberies, muggings."

"It's not the same."

"Maggie, she's just doing her job."

"I know. I'm sorry. I know." She covered her face with her hands, drew air in, slowly let it out. "I've got the shakes, that's all. I don't want to stay here tonight."

"We don't have to. We'll go to a hotel. How much more do you need, Detective…was it Fletcher?"

"Yes. Just a few more questions. You said both of you were out all evening."

"Yeah, Maggie won a case today, and we decided to go out and celebrate. She's been piled under for more than a month. We went to the Starfire club with some friends." As he spoke, he rubbed soothing circles over his wife's back. "Drinks, dinner, a little dancing. Like we told the other policeman, we didn't get home until nearly two."

"Does anyone other than the two of you have a key?"

"Our housekeeper."

"Would she also have the security code?"

"Sure." Joe started to speak, then blinked,

stuttered. "Oh listen, Carol's been cleaning for us for nearly ten years. She's practically family."

"It's just procedure, Mr. Chambers. Could I have her full name and address, for the record?"

She took them through the entire evening, looking for a connection, a contact, anything that struck a chord. But for the Chamberses it had been nothing more than an entertaining evening out, until they'd walked back in their own front door.

When Ally left them, she had a partial list of stolen items, with a promise for the complete as well as the insurance information. The crime scene unit was still working, but she'd gone over the scene herself. She didn't expect the miracle of fingerprints or dropped clues.

The moon had set, but the stars were out and brilliant. The wind had picked up to dance down the street in little whirls and gusts. The neighborhood was hushed, the houses dark. Those who lived here had long since been tucked in for the night.

She doubted the canvass was going to turn up any handy eyewitnesses.

Jonah was leaning against the hood of his car,

drinking what appeared to be a cup of takeout coffee with one of the uniforms.

When she approached the car, Jonah held out the half cup he had left. "Thanks."

"You can have a whole one. There's a twenty-four-hour place a few blocks down."

"This is fine," she replied, taking the cup. "Officer, you and your partner were first on scene?"

"Yes, ma'am."

"I'll need your report on my desk by eleven hundred." With a brisk nod, the officer headed for his car. Ally sipped the coffee, then turned to Jonah and handed him the cup. "You didn't have to wait. I can get a ride home in one of the radio cars."

"I have a stake here." He opened the car door. "Were they at my place?"

"Now why would you ask me when we both know you just got finished pumping that uniform?"

"Hey, I bought the coffee." He handed it back to her, then walked around to the driver's side.

"So, the perps picked their marks at the Starfire tonight. Have they hit there before?"

"No, you're still the only repeater. They'll come back to you." She shut her exhausted eyes. "It's just a matter of time."

"Well that makes me feel lots better. What kind of take did they get?"

"BMW roadster out of the garage, some art, high end electronics and heavy on the jewelry."

"Don't these people have safes?"

"These did, a small one in the walk-in closet of the master suite. Of course they had the combination for it written down on a piece of paper in the desk."

"That'll discourage the criminal element."

"They had a security system, which they swear they engaged when they left—though the wife didn't look quite so sure of that. Anyway, the point is they felt secure. Nice house, nice neighborhood. People get sloppy." Eyes still closed, she circled her head, cracking out the tension. "They're both lawyers."

"Well, hell then, what do we care?"

She was tired enough to laugh. "Watch it, ace. My aunt's district attorney in Urbana."

"You going to drink that coffee or just hold on to it?"

"What? Oh, no, here, I don't want anymore. It'll just keep me awake."

He doubted a tanker truck of coffee could keep her awake much longer. Her voice was going thick, adding, he thought, to the in-the-gut sexiness of it. Fatigue had her unguarded enough to tilt her face toward him as she tried to find a comfortable resting spot. Her eyes were shut, her lips soft and just parted.

He had a feeling he knew exactly how they'd taste. Warm and soft. Ripe with sleep.

At a stop sign, he put the car in neutral, engaged the emergency brake, then leaned over her to press the mechanism that lowered her seat-back.

She jerked up, rapped her head smartly against his. Even as he swore she slapped a hand on his chest.

"Back off!"

"Relax, Fletcher, I'm not jumping you. I like

my women awake when we make love. I'm putting your seat back. If you're going to sleep, you might as well get as close to horizontal as we can manage."

"I'm all right." Mortified, but all right, she thought. "I wasn't sleeping."

He put a hand on her forehead, shoved her back. "Shut up, Allison."

"I wasn't sleeping. I was thinking."

"Think tomorrow. You're brain-dead." He glanced over at her as he started to drive again. "How many hours have you been on duty?"

"That's math, I can't do math if I'm brain-dead." She gave up and yawned. "I'm on eight to fours."

"It's closing in on 4:00 a.m., that gives you twenty hours. Why don't you put in for night shift until this is over, or do you have a death wish?"

"It's not my only case." She'd already decided to talk to her lieutenant. She couldn't give her best to the job on a couple of hours sleep a night. But it wasn't any of Jonah's business how she ran her life.

"I guess Denver's not safe without you on the job."

She might have been tired, but she still had a pretty good ear for sarcasm. "That's right, Blackhawk. Without my watchful eye, the city's in chaos. It's a heavy burden but, well, somebody's got to shoulder it. Just pull up at the corner. My building's only a half a block down."

He ignored her, drove through the light and pulled smoothly to the curb in front of her building. "Okay. Thanks." She reached down to retrieve her bag from the floor.

He was already out of the car, skirting around the hood. Maybe it was fatigue that had her reacting so slowly, as if she were moving through syrup instead of air. But he had the outside handle of the door seconds before she had the inside handle.

For about five seconds they battled for control. Then with a halfhearted snarl, Ally let him open the door for her. "What are you, from another century? Do I look incapable of operating the complex mechanism of a car door?"

"No. You look tired."

"Well, I am. So good night."

"I'll walk you up."

"Get a grip."

But he fell into step beside her, and damn him, reached the door one pace ahead of her. Saying nothing, merely watching her with those impossibly clear green eyes, he held it open for her.

"I'll have to curtsy in a minute," she muttered under her breath.

He grinned at her back, then crossed to the lobby elevators with her, sliding his hands into his pockets.

"I can make it from here."

"I'll take you to your door."

"It's not a damn date."

"Lack of sleep's making you irritable." He stepped into the elevator with her. "No, wait, you're always irritable. My mistake."

"I don't like you." She jabbed the button for the fourth floor.

"Thank God you cleared that up. I was afraid you were falling for me."

The movement of the elevator tipped her

already shaky balance. She swayed, and he closed a hand over her arm.

"Cut it out."

"No."

She jerked at her arm. He tightened his grip. "Don't embarrass yourself, Fletcher. You're asleep on your feet. What's your apartment number?"

He was right, and it was stupid to pretend otherwise, and foolish to take it out on him. "Four-oh-nine. Let me go, will you? I'll be all right after a couple hours' sleep."

"I don't doubt it." But he held on to her when the elevator opened.

"You're not coming in."

"Well, there go my plans to toss you over my shoulder, dump you in bed and have my wicked way with you. Next time. Key?"

"What?"

Her burnt-honey eyes were blurry, the delicate skin beneath them bruised. The wave of tenderness that swept inside him was a complete surprise, and far from comfortable. "Honey, give me your key."

"Oh. I'm punchy." She dug it out of her jacket pocket. "And don't call me honey."

"I meant Detective Honey." He heard her snicker as he unlocked her door. He pulled the key back out of the lock, took her hand, dropped it in and closed her fingers around it. "Good night."

"Yeah. Thanks for the lift." Because it seemed the thing to do, she closed the door in his face.

Hell of a face, she thought as she stumbled toward the bedroom. Face that dangerous ought to be registered as a weapon. A woman who trusted a face like that got exactly what she deserved.

And probably enjoyed every minute of it.

Ally stripped off her jacket, whimpering a little as she pried off her shoes. She set her alarm, then fell facedown and fully clothed on the bed. And was instantly asleep.

Four and a half hours later, she was finishing up her morning meeting in the conference room at her station house. And her fourth cup of coffee.

"We'll canvass the neighborhood," Ally

said, "We could get lucky. In that kind of development, people tend to look out for each
other. Some sort of vehicle was necessary to
get the perpetrators to the Chamberses', and to
transport at least some of the stolen goods. The
sports car they boosted wouldn't hold that
much. We have a full description of the car, and
the APB's out on it."

Lieutenant Kiniki nodded. He was a toughly
built man in his mid-forties who enjoyed the
way command sat on his shoulders. "The
Starfire's a new pool for them. I want two men
over there to check out the setup. Soft clothes,"
he added, indicating he wanted his detectives to
dress casually rather than in suit jackets. "Let's
keep it low-key."

"Hickman and Carson are canvassing pawn
shops, pressuring known fences." Ally glanced
toward her two associates.

"Nothing there." Hickman lifted his hands.
"Lydia and I've got a couple of good sources,
and we've put the heat on. Nobody knows
anything. My take is that whoever's running this
has an outside channel."

"Keep the heat on," Kiniki ordered. "What about the insurance angle."

"It doesn't play out," Ally told him. "We've got nine hits and five different insurance companies. We're still trying to find a connection, but so far that's a dead end. We've got no common links between the victims that carry through," she went on. "Out of the nine, we've got four different banks, three different brokerage houses, nine different doctors, nine different places of employment."

She rubbed the ache at the back of her neck and went down her list. "Two of the women go to the same hair salon—different operators, different schedules. They use different cleaning services, different mechanics. Now two of the targets used the same caterer in the last six months, and we're running that. But it doesn't look like a hook. The only common link so far is a night on the town."

"Give me the rundown on Blackhawk's," Kiniki ordered.

"The place does a hell of a business," Ally began. "Pulls in a big crowd, and the crowd varies, though it's heavy on the upwardly mobile. Couples, singles on the prowl, groups. He's got good security."

Absently Ally rubbed her eyes, then remembered herself and lowered them. "He's got cameras, and I'm working on getting the security tapes. Sloan is the floater. He works the public areas, has access to everything. There are six tables in the bar area and thirty-two in the club. People push them together if they get friendly. There's a coat check but not everybody bothers with it. I couldn't count the number of handbags left on tables when the dancing started."

"People mill," Lydia added. "Especially the younger customers. It's a regular meeting ground for them, and they tend to table hop. Lots of sex vibes." She gave Hickman a bland look when he chortled. "It's a sexy place. People get careless when their blood's hot. There's a ripple when Blackhawk comes through."

"A ripple?" Hickman repeated. "Is that a technical term?"

"The women watch him. They don't watch their bags."

"That's accurate." Ally walked over to the board where the list of victims and stolen items were posted. "Every hit involved a woman. There are no single men on the list. The female's the prime target. What's a woman carry in her purse?"

"That," Hickman said, "is one of life's most complex mysteries."

"Her keys," Ally continued. "Her wallet—with ID, credit cards. Pictures of her kids if she has them. None of the victims had children at home. If we break this down to its basic element, we're looking first for a pickpocket. Somebody with good fingers who can get what he needs out of a bag, then put it back before the victim knows she's been hit. Do an imprint of the key, make a copy."

"If you pick the pocket, why put the stuff back?" Hickman asked.

"Keep the victim unaware, buy more time. A woman goes into the bathroom, she takes her purse. If she reaches in for her lipstick and doesn't find her wallet, she's going to send up an alarm. This way, the house is hit and the perpetrators are out before the victims get home. Whatever time they get home."

She turned back to the board. "Twelve-thirty, one-fifteen, twelve-ten, and so on. Somebody at the club alerts the burglars when the victims call for their check. Somebody's on the inside, or a regular and repeat customer. At Blackhawk's the average time between calling for the check and leaving the club was about twenty minutes."

"We have two other clubs involved now, besides Blackhawk's." Kiniki's brow furrowed. "We'll need stakeouts on all of them."

"Yes, sir. But Blackhawk's is where they'll come back. That's the money tree."

"Find a way to cut down the tree, Fletcher." He got to his feet. "And take some personal time today. Get some sleep."

She took him up on it and curled up on the small sofa in the coffee room, leaving word that she was to be notified when the reports she was waiting for came in.

She got ninety minutes and felt very close to human when Hickman shook her shoulder.

"Did you steal my cheese bagel?"

"What?" She pushed herself up, shoved back her hair.

"You like cheese bagels. I had one. It's gone. I'm detecting."

Shaking off sleep, she dug her clip out of her pocket and pulled back her hair. "It didn't have your name on it."

"Did, too."

She circled her shoulders. "Is your name Pineview Bakery? Besides I only ate half of it." She checked her watch. "The first on scene reports in yet?"

"Yeah, and so's your warrant."

"Great." She swung to her feet, adjusted her weapon harness. "I'll be in the field."

"I want a cheese bagel back in that box by end of shift."

"I only ate half of it," she called out and stopped by her desk for the paperwork. Scanning it, ignoring the backwash of noise from the detectives' bullpen, she hitched her harness into a more comfortable position, then shrugged into her jacket.

She glanced up when the noise became a

murmur, and watched her father walk in. Like Blackhawk, she thought, this was a man who created ripples.

She knew a few of her fellow officers harbored some resentment over her rapid rise to detective. There were mutters now and then, just loud enough for her to hear, about favoritism and oiling the ranks.

She'd earned her badge, and knew it. Ally was too proud of her father, and too secure in her own abilities to let mutters worry her.

"Commissioner."

"Detective. Got a minute?"

"A couple." She pulled her shoulder bag from her bottom desk drawer. "Can we walk and talk? I'm on my way out. Got a warrant to serve on Jonah Blackhawk."

"Ah." He stepped back to let her pass, and his eyes scanned the room. If there were any mutters, they would wait until he was well out of range.

"Stairs okay with you?" she asked. "I didn't have time to work out this morning."

"I think I can keep up with you. What's the warrant?"

"To confiscate and view Blackhawk's security tapes. He got pissy about it yesterday. I seem to put his back up."

Boyd pushed open the door to the stairwell, then angled his head to study his daughter's back as she passed through. "I seem to detect a few ruffled feathers on yours."

"Okay, good eye. We put each other's backs up."

"I figured you would. You both like to do things your own way."

"Why would I want to do them someone else's way?"

"Exactly." Boyd skimmed a hand down the long, sleek tail of her hair. His little girl had always had a mind of her own, and a very hard head around it. "Speaking of ruffled feathers, I have a meeting with the mayor in an hour."

"Better you than me," Ally said cheerfully as she jogged down the stairs.

"What can you tell me about last night's break-in?"

"Same MO. They hit a real treasure trove with the Chamberses. Mrs. Chambers got me the loss list this morning. The woman's efficient. They were fully insured—value of stolen items comes to a solid two hundred and twenty-five thousand."

"That's the biggest haul so far."

"Yeah. I'm hoping it makes them cocky. They took some art this time. I don't know if it was dumb luck or somebody knew what they had when they saw it. They have to have somewhere to keep the goods before they turn them. Big enough for a car."

"A decent chop shop could have a car dismantled and turned in a couple hours."

"Yeah, but…" She started to push open the next door herself, but her father beat her to it. It reminded her oddly, and not entirely happily, of Jonah.

"But?" he prompted as they crossed the lobby.

"I don't think that's the route. Somebody likes nice things. Somebody has really good taste. At the second hit, they took a collection of rare books, but they left an antique clock. It was appraised at five thousand, but it was dead ugly. It's like they said, please, don't insult us. There've been other cars at other scenes, but they've only taken two. Cool cars."

"Burglars with standards."

"Yeah, I think so." When they stepped outside she blinked against the brilliant sunlight until she pulled out her shaded glasses. "And a kind of arrogance. Arrogance is a mistake. That's going to turn it my way."

"I hope so. The pressure's on, Ally." He walked her to her car, opened the door for her in a way that made her frown and think of Jonah again. "We're getting press, the kind that makes the mayor uncomfortable."

"In my best judgment they won't wait more than a week. They're rolling now. They'll come back to Blackhawk's."

"They got a bigger slice of pie from the new place."

"Blackhawk's is reliable. Once I spend a few nights under there, I'll start recognizing faces. I'll pin him, Dad."

"I believe it." He bent down to kiss her cheek. "And I'll handle the mayor."

"I believe it." She slid behind the wheel. "Question."

"Ask it."

"You've known Jonah Blackhawk for what, like fifteen years?"

"Seventeen."

"How come you never had him over to the house? You know for dinner or football afternoons or one of your world famous cookouts?"

"He wouldn't come. Always acknowledged the invitation, thanked me and said he was busy."

"Seventeen years." Idly she tapped her fingers on the steering wheel. "That's a lot of busy. Well, some people don't like socializing with cops."

"Some people," Boyd told her, "draw lines and never believe they have the right to cross them. He'd meet me at the station house." The memory made Boyd grin. "He didn't like it, but he'd do it. He'd meet me for coffee or a beer, at the gym. But he'd never come to my home. He'd consider that crossing the line. I've never convinced him otherwise."

"Funny, he strikes me as being a man who considers himself good enough for anything, or anyone."

"There are a lot of twists and pockets in Jonah. And very little about him that's simple."

Chapter 4

She called ahead, and had to admit she was surprised when Jonah answered the phone in his office.

"It's Fletcher. I didn't think you were much on daylight hours."

"I'm not. Some days are exceptions. What can I do for you, Detective?"

"You can come downstairs and let me in. I'll be there in ten minutes."

"I'm not going anywhere." He waited a beat. "So, what are you wearing?"

She hated herself for laughing, and hoped she managed to smother most of it. "My badge," she told him, and flicked the phone off.

Jonah hung up, sat back and entertained himself by imagining Allison Fletcher wearing her badge, and nothing else. The image came through, entirely too clear, entirely too appealing, and had him shoving back from the desk.

He had no business imagining Boyd's daughter naked. No business, he reminded himself, fantasizing about Boyd's daughter in any way whatsoever. Or wondering how her mouth would taste. Or what scent he'd find on the flesh just under the line of that very stubborn jaw.

God, he wanted to sink his teeth there, right there. Just once.

Forbidden fruit, he told himself and paced since there was no one to see. She was forbidden fruit and therefore all the more alluring. She wasn't even his type. Maybe he liked leggy blondes. Maybe he liked leggy blondes with brains and a strong backbone. But he preferred friendlier women.

Friendlier, unarmed women, he thought, amusing himself.

He hadn't been able to get her out of his head, and the clearest most compelling picture had been the yielding and temporary, he was certain, fragility of her when she'd fallen asleep in his car.

Well, he'd always been a sucker for the needy, he reminded himself, as he pulled up the blinds on his office window. Which should solve his problem over Allison. Despite that short interlude of vulnerability early that morning, needy was one thing the gorgeous detective wasn't.

She had a use for him, again temporary. And when the job was done, they'd both go back to their separate corners in their separate worlds. And that would be the end of that.

He saw her pull up in front of the club. At least she'd had the sense to drive, he noted, and wasn't hiking all over Denver today.

He took his time going down to let her in.

"Good morning, Detective." He looked around her, studied the flashy lines of the classic red-and-white Stingray. "Nice car. Is that the new police issue? Oh wait, what was I thinking? Your daddy's loaded."

"If you think you can razz me over a car, you're going to be disappointed. Nobody razzes like a precinct full of cops."

"I'll practice. Nice threads," he commented and rubbed the lapel of her subtly patterned brown jacket between his thumb and forefinger. "Very nice."

"So we both like Italian designers. We can compare wardrobes later."

Because he knew it would irritate her, because he enjoyed the way the gold highlighted her eyes when he irritated her, he shifted, blocking her before she could step inside. "Let me see the badge."

"Come off it, Blackhawk."

"No. Let's see it."

Eyes narrowed behind her sunglasses, she pulled her badge out of her pocket, pushed it close to his face. "See it?"

"Yes. Badge number 31628. I'll buy myself a lottery ticket and play your numbers."

"Here's something else you might want to look at." She took out the warrant, held it up.

"Fast work." He'd expected no less. "Come on up. I've been reviewing the tapes. You look rested," he said as they walked to his elevator.

"I am."

"Any progress?"

"The investigation is ongoing."

"Hmm, policy line." He gestured her into the elevator. "We seem to be spending a lot of time in these. Close quarters."

"You could do your heart a favor and take the stairs."

"My heart's never caused me any problems. How about yours?"

"Whole and healthy, thanks." She walked out when the doors opened. "Wow, you actually let the sunlight in here. I'm shocked. Let's have the tapes. I'll give a receipt."

She wasn't wearing perfume today, he noted. Just soap and skin. Odd how erotic that simplicity could be. "In a hurry?"

"Clock's ticking."

He strolled into an adjoining room. After a small internal battle, Ally walked over to the doorway. It was a small bedroom. Small, she noted, because it was two-thirds bed. A black pool of bed, unframed and on a raised platform.

Curious, she looked up and was mildly disappointed there wasn't a mirror on the ceiling.

"It would be too obvious," Jonah told her when her gaze skimmed back to his.

"The bed's already a statement. An obvious one."

"But not vain."

"Hmm." To amuse herself she poked around the room. On the walls were a number of framed black-and-white photographs. Arty, interesting, and all stark or shadowy night scenes.

She recognized a couple of the artists, pursed her lips. So the man had a good eye for art, and decent taste, she admitted.

"I've got this print." She tapped a finger against a study of an ancient man in a ragged straw hat sleeping on a cracked concrete stoop, a paper bag still clutched in his hand. "Shade Colby. I like his work."

"So do I. And his wife's. Bryan Mitchell. That's one of hers beside it. The old couple holding hands on the bench at the bus stop."

"Quite a contrast, despair and hope."

"Life's full of both."

"Apparently."

She wandered. There was a closet, closed, an exit door, securely locked, and what she assumed was a bath or washroom just beyond. She thought of the sex vibes Lydia Carson had referred to. Oh, yeah, this room had plenty of them. It all but smoked with them.

"So, what's through there?" She jerked a thumb at another door. Instead of answering he gestured, inviting her to see for herself.

She opened the door, let out a long sigh of pleasure. "Now we're talking." The fully equipped gym was a great deal more appealing to her than a lake-size bed.

He watched as she trailed her fingers over machines, picked up free weights, doing a few absent curls as she roamed. Very telling, he thought, that she'd given the bed a sneer, and was all but dewy-eyed over his Nautilus.

"You got a sauna?" Envy curled inside her as she pressed her nose to a little window of a wooden door and peered into the room beyond.

"Want to try it out?"

She turned her head enough to slide her gaze in his direction. And the sneer was back. "This is pretty elaborate when you could be at a full-service health club in two minutes."

"Health clubs have members—that's the first strike. They also have regular hours. Strike two. And I don't like using someone else's equipment."

"Strike three. You're a very particular man, Blackhawk."

"That's right." He took a bottle of water out of a clear-fronted bar fridge. "Want one?"

"No." She replaced the free weight, moved back to the doorway. "Well, thanks for the tour. Now, the tapes, Blackhawk."

"Yeah, clock's ticking." He unscrewed the top of the bottle, took a casual sip. "You know what I like about night work, Detective Fletcher?"

She looked deliberately toward the bed, then back at him. "Oh, I think I can figure it out."

"Well, there's that, but what I really like about night work is that it's always whatever time you want it to be. My favorite's the three o'clock hour. For most people, that's the hard time. If they don't sleep through it, that's the time the mind wakes up and starts worrying about what they did or didn't do that day, or what they'll do or not do the next. And the next, and right up until life's over."

"And you don't worry about yesterday or tomorrow."

"You miss a lot of the now doing that. There's only so much now to go around."

"I don't have a lot of the now to stand around philosophizing with you."

"Take a minute." He crossed to her, leaning on one jamb as she leaned on the other. "A lot of people who come into my place are night people—or those who want to remember when they were. Most have jobs now, the kind of jobs that pay well and make them responsible citizens."

She took the water bottle from his hand, drank. "Your job pays well."

He grinned. That quick jab was just one of the things that attracted him to her. "You saying I'm not a responsible citizen? My lawyers and accountants would disagree. However, my point is that people come in here to forget about their responsibilities for a while. To forget the clock's ticking and they have to punch in at 9:00 a.m. I give them a place without clocks—at least till last call."

"And this means?" She passed the bottle back to him.

"Forget about the facts a minute. Look at the shadows. You're hunting night people."

And he was one of them, she thought. Very much one of the night people, with his black mane of hair and cool, cat's eyes. "I'm not arguing with that."

"But are you thinking like them? They've picked their prey, and when they move, they move fast. It would be less risky, give them more time to study the lay of the land, if they waited to make the hit during the day. Stake out the mark, learn their patterns—when do they leave for the office, when do they get back? These guys could probably nail it down in a couple of days."

He lifted the bottle, drank. "That would be more efficient. Why don't they play it that way?"

"Because they're arrogant."

"Yeah, but that's only the top layer. Go down."

"They like the kick, the rush."

"Exactly. They're hungry, and they like the thrill of working in the dark."

It irked almost as much as it intrigued her that his thought process so closely followed her own. "You think that hasn't occurred to me before?"

"I figure it has, but I wonder if you've factored in that people who live at night are always more dangerous than people who live during the day."

"Does that include you?"

"Damn right."

"So warned." She started to turn away, then stopped, stared down at the hand he'd shot out to grip her arm. "What's your problem, Blackhawk?"

"I haven't figured it out yet. Why didn't you send a uniform over here to pick up the tapes?"

"Because it's my case."

"No."

"No, it's not my case?"

"No, that's not the reason. I'm crowding

you." He edged forward to prove it. "Why haven't you decked me?"

"I don't make a habit of punching out civilians." She angled her chin when he nudged her back against the doorjamb. "But I can make an exception."

"Your pulse is jumping."

"It tends to when I'm irritated." Aroused, she'd nearly said aroused because that was the word that came into her head. That was the sensation sliding through her body. And enough was enough.

She shifted, a smooth move that should have planted her elbow in his gut and moved him aside. But he countered, just as smoothly, and changed his grip so that his fingers wrapped tight around her wrist. Instinctively she pivoted, started to hook her foot behind his to take him down.

He adjusted his weight, used it to plaster her back against the door. She told herself it was annoyance that quickened her breathing, and not the way the lines of his body pressed against the lines of hers.

She bunched the hand at her side into a fist, calculated the wisdom of using it for one short-armed punch to the face, and decided sarcasm was a more potent weapon against him.

"Next time, ask me if I want to dance. I'm not in the mood to—" She broke off when she saw something sharp come into his eyes, something reckless that had her already rapid pulse tripping to a faster rate.

She forgot self-defense, forgot the fist she still held ready. "Damn it, Blackhawk, back off. What do you want from me?"

"The hell with it." He forgot the rules, forgot the consequences of breaking them. All he could see was her. "The hell with it, let's find out."

He let the bottle drop, and the water that remained in it spilled unnoticed on the bedroom rug. He wanted his hands on her, both his hands, and used them to hold her arms over her head as his mouth came down on hers.

He felt her body jerk against his. Protest or invitation, he didn't care. One way or the other, he was bound to be damned for this single outrageous act. So he might as well make the most of it.

He used his teeth on her, the way he'd already imagined, scraping them along the long line of her lower lip. Freeing the warmth, the softness of it to him, then absorbing it. She made some sound, something that seemed to claw up from her throat and was every bit as primitive as the need that raged through him.

The scent of her—cool soap and skin—the flavor of her, such a contrast of ripeness and heat, overwhelmed him, stirred every hunger he'd ever known.

When his hands took her, fingers sliding down, gripping her hips, he was ready to feed those hungers, to take what he craved without a second thought.

Then his hand bumped over her weapon.

He jerked back as if she'd drawn it and shot him.

What was he doing? What in God's name was he doing?

She said nothing, only stared at him with eyes that had gone blurry at the edges. Her arms remained over her head, as if his hands still pinned them there.

Her body quaked.

"That was a mistake," she managed to say.

"I know it."

"A really serious mistake."

With her eyes open, she fisted her hands in his hair and dragged his mouth back to hers.

This time it was his body that jerked, and the shock of it vibrated through her, down to the bone. He'd savaged her mouth with that first mad kiss, and she wanted him to do it again. He would damn well do it again until her system stopped screaming.

She couldn't breathe without breathing him, and every desperate gulp of air was like the pump of a drug. The power of it charged through her while their lips and tongues warred.

With one violent move, he yanked her shirt out of the waistband of her slacks, then snaked his hand beneath, until it closed over her breast.

The groan came from both of them.

"The minute I saw you." He tore his mouth from hers to feast on her throat. "The first minute I saw you."

"I know." She wanted his mouth again, had to have it. "I know."

He started to drag her jacket off, had it halfway down her arms when sanity began to pound against madness. The madness urged him to take her—why shouldn't he?—fast and hard. To take what he needed, the way he needed it, and please himself.

"Ally." He said her name, and the old-fashioned sweetness of it clicked reality back into place.

She saw him step back—though he didn't move, she saw the deliberate distance he built between them by the change in his eyes. Those fascinating and clear green eyes.

"Okay." She sucked in a breath. "Okay, okay." In an almost absent move she patted his shoulder until he did indeed step back. "That was…whoa." She sidestepped, paced away into his office. "Okay, that was…something."

"Something or other."

"I need a minute for my mind to clear." She'd never had passion slam into her with a force that blanked the mind. But she'd have to worry about that, deal with that later. Right now it was essential she find her balance.

"We probably both knew that was in there. And it's probably best we got it out," she said.

To give himself a moment he bent down,

picked up the empty water bottle, set it aside. Then he dipped his hands into his pockets because they weren't altogether steady, and followed her into the office.

"I'll agree with the first part and reserve judgment on the second. What do we do now?"

"Now we...get over it."

Just like that? he thought. She'd cut him off at the knees, and now he was supposed to just hobble away and get over it?

"Fine." Pride iced his voice. He walked over, took three tapes out of his desk drawer. "I believe these satisfy your warrant."

Her palms were sweaty, but she couldn't sacrifice the dignity she was trying to rebuild by wiping them off. She took the tapes, slipped them into her shoulder bag. "I'll give you a receipt."

"Forget it."

"I'll give you a receipt," she repeated, and took out a pad. "It's procedure."

"We wouldn't want to tamper with procedure." He held out his hand, accepting the copy she offered. "Don't let me keep you, Fletcher. Clock's ticking."

She strode to the door, yanked it open. Dignity be damned, she decided and spun back. "You can save the attitude. You made the first move, I made the second. That's an even slate to me, and now it's done."

"Honey—make that Detective Honey, if we were done, we'd both be feeling a lot better right now."

"Yeah, well. We'll live with it," she muttered and sacrificed dignity for satisfaction by slamming the door.

Ally wasn't cut out to be a waitress. She was sure of it when, during her second shift at Blackhawk's, she poured the drink Beth had allowed her to serve over the head of the idiot customer who grabbed her butt and invited her to engage in a sexual act that was illegal in several states.

The customer had objected, rather strongly, to her response, but before she could flatten him, Will had appeared like smoke between them. She'd had to stand passively and be rescued.

It had grated for hours.

But if she was sure of her lack of waitress potential after her second shift, she was desperate to shed her cover by the third.

She wanted action. And not the kind that required her to serve wild wings in demon sauce and take orders for drinks called tornadoes to young executives on the make.

Twenty minutes into her third night at Blackhawk's had given her a profound respect for those who served and cleared and tolerated impatience, lousy tips and lewd propositions.

"I hate people." Ally waited for her drink order at the bar while Pete drew a beer off tap.

"Ah, no, you don't."

"Yes. Yes, I do. I really do. They're rude, annoying, oblivious. And all of them are jammed into Blackhawk's."

"And it's only six-thirty."

"Please. Six thirty-five. Every minute counts." She glanced back at Jan who worked the bar area, all but dancing between tables as she cleared, served and played up her assets. "How does she do it?"

"Some are born for it, Blondie. You'll excuse

my saying so, but you're not. Not that you don't do the job, but you don't have the passion."

She rolled her eyes. "I don't have the arches, either." She started to lift the tray, eyes tracking the room as always, then she let it drop again when she spotted the man coming in the front door.

"Oh, hell. Pete, ask Jan to get this order to table eight club side. I have to do something."

"Ally, what're you doing here?"

It was all Dennis got out of his mouth before Ally grabbed his arm and hauled him through the bar, into the kitchen and out the back door. "Damn it, Dennis. Damn it!"

"What's the matter? What did you drag me out here for?" He put on his best baffled look, but she'd seen it before. She'd seen the whole routine before.

"I'm on the job. You'll blow my cover, for God's sake. I told you what would happen if you started following me again."

"I don't know what you're talking about." His injured air had worked on her once. More than once.

"You listen to me." She stepped close, jabbed a

finger in his chest. "Listen hard, Dennis. We're done. We have been done for months. There's no chance that's going to change, and every chance, if you keep hassling me, I'll slap a restraining order on your butt and make your life a living hell."

His mouth thinned, his eyebrows lowered, the way she knew they did when he was backed into a corner. "This is a public place. All I did was walk into a public place. I'm entitled to buy a drink in a bar when I'm in the mood."

"You're not entitled to follow me, or to jeopardize my cover in a police investigation. You crossed the line, and I'm calling the D.A.'s office in the morning."

"You don't have to do that. Come on, Ally. How was I supposed to know you were on the job here? I just happened to pass by and—"

"Don't lie to me." She balled her hand into a fist, then in frustration tapped it against her own temple as she turned away. "Don't lie."

"I just miss you so much. I think about you all the time. I can't help it. I know I shouldn't have followed you. I didn't mean to. I was just hoping we could talk, that's all. Come on, baby."

He took her shoulders, buried his face in her hair in a way that made her skin crawl. "If we could just talk."

"Don't…touch me." She hunched her shoulders, started to pull away, but he wrapped his arms around her, one hard squeeze of possession.

"Don't pull away. You know it makes me crazy when you go cold like that."

She could have had him flat on his back with her foot on his throat in two moves. She didn't want it to come to that. "Dennis, don't make me hurt you. Just leave me alone. Take your hands off me and leave me alone or it's going to be so much worse than it already is."

"No. It'll be better. I swear, it'll be better. You just have to take me back, and things'll be the way they used to be."

"No. They won't." She stiffened, braced to break the hold. "Let me go."

Light spilled out of the kitchen door as it opened. "I'd advise you to do what the lady asked," Jonah warned. "And do it fast."

She closed her eyes, felt temper and embarrassment rise up under the frustration. "I can handle this."

"Maybe, but you won't. This is my place. Take your hands off her."

"We're having a private conversation." Dennis turned, but pulled Ally with him.

"Not anymore. Go inside, Ally."

"This is none of your business." Dennis's voice rose, cracked. It was a tenor she'd heard before. "Just butt out."

"That wasn't the right response."

She moved now, breaking free and stepping between the men when Jonah moved forward. There was a gleam in his eye that worried her, like a flash of lightning against thin ice. "Don't. Please."

Anger wouldn't have stopped him, nor would an order. But the plea in her eyes, the weariness in them, did. "Go back inside," he said again, but quietly as he laid a hand on her shoulder.

"So that's the way it is." Dennis lifted bunched fists. "There's nobody else. That's what you told me. No, there was nobody else. Just another lie. Just one more of your lies. You've been sleeping with him all along, haven't you? Lying bitch."

Jonah moved like a snake. She'd seen street fights before. Had broken up her share while in uniform. She only had time to swear and leap forward, but Jonah already had Dennis up against the wall.

"Stop it," she said again and grabbed his arm to try to pull him off. She might as well have tried to shove aside a mountain.

He shot her one steely look. "No." He said it casually, like a shrug. Then he plowed his fist into Dennis's belly. "I don't like men who push women around or call them names." His voice stayed cool and steady as he delivered a second blow. "I won't tolerate it in my place. You got that?"

He let go, stepped back, and Dennis collapsed in a heap at his feet. "I think he got it."

"Great. Wonderful." While Dennis moaned, Ally pressed her fingers to her eyes. "You just gut-punched an assistant district attorney."

"And your point would be?"

"Help me get him up."

"No." Before she could try to haul Dennis to

his feet, Jonah took her arm. "He walked in on his own, he'll walk away on his own."

"I can't leave him here, curled up like a damn shrimp on the pavement."

"He'll get up. Right, Dennis?" Elegant and unruffled in black, Jonah crouched down beside the groaning man. "You're going to get up, you're going to walk away. And you're not going to come back here in this lifetime. You're going to stay very far away from Allison. In fact, if you find out that by some mischance you're breathing the same air, you'll hold your breath and run in the opposite direction."

Dennis struggled to his hands and knees, retched. Tears swam in his eyes, but behind them was a rage that drilled in his head like a diamond bit. "You're welcome to her." Pain radiated through him as he stumbled to his feet. "She'll use you, then toss you aside. Just like she did me. You're welcome to her," he repeated, then limped away.

"Looks like you're all mine now." Jonah straightened, flicked fingers down his shirt as if removing some pesky lint. "But if you're going to start using me, I'd prefer we do it inside."

"It's not funny."

"No." He studied her face, the shadowed eyes and the pity in them. "I can see that. I'm sorry. Why don't you come inside, take a few minutes up in my office until you're feeling steadier."

"I'm okay." But she turned away, dragged the clip out of her hair as if it were suddenly too tight. "I don't want to talk about it now."

"All right." He put his hands on her shoulders, used his thumbs to press at the tension. "Take a minute anyway."

"I hate having him touch me, and I feel lousy because I hate it. I don't think it jeopardized the cover."

"No. According to Pete, some dude walked in, you flipped and dragged him out."

"Anybody asks, I'll keep it close to the truth. Ex-boyfriend who's hassling me."

"Then stop worrying." He turned her around. "And stop feeling guilty. You're not responsible for other people's feelings."

"Sure you are, when you help make them.

Anyway." She lifted a hand to the one he still rested on her shoulder, patted it. "Thanks. I could have handled him, but thanks."

"You're welcome."

He couldn't stop himself from leaning into her, drawing her close. He watched her lashes lower, her mouth lift to his. And was a breath away from tasting her when the light spilled over them.

"Oh. Sorry." Frannie stood, framed in the door where kitchen noise clattered, a lighter in one hand, a cigarette at the ready in the other.

"No." Ally broke away, furious with herself for forgetting her priorities. "I was just going back in. I'm already late." She flicked one look at Jonah then hurried back inside.

Frannie waited until the door swung shut, then stepped over to lean back against the wall. She flicked on her lighter. "Well," she said.

"Well."

She blew out smoke on a sigh. "She's beautiful."

"Yes, she is."

"Smart, too. It comes across."

"Yeah."

"Just your type."

This time he angled his head. "You think so?"

"Sure." The tip of her cigarette glowed as she lifted it to her lips. "Classy. Class shows. She suits you."

It troubled him, more than he'd imagined it would, to dance around the truth with an old friend. "We'll see how well we fit."

Frannie moved a shoulder. But she'd already seen. They fit like lock and key. "Was there trouble with that suit?"

Jonah glanced in the direction Dennis had taken. "Nothing major. An ex who doesn't like being an ex."

"Figured it was something like that. Well, if it matters, I like her."

"It matters, Frannie." He walked to her, touched a hand to her cheek. "You matter, and always have."

Chapter 5

Six days after the Chamberses' burglary, Ally stood in her lieutenant's office. To save time, she'd already changed into her waitress gear for the evening. She had her badge in the pocket of her trousers and her clutch piece strapped just above her ankle.

"We haven't been able to trace one single piece of stolen property." She knew it wasn't what he wanted to hear. "There's no news on the street. Even Hickman's bottomless sources are dry. Whoever's pushing the buttons on this is smart, private and patient."

"You've been inside Blackhawk's for a week."

"Yes, sir. I can't tell you any more than I could the first day. Between the security tapes and my own in-the-field observations I've tagged several regulars. But nobody pops. On the upside, my cover's secure."

"Fortunately. Shut the door, Detective."

Her stomach sank a little, but she did so, and stood in the glass box of his office with the noise from the bullpen humming behind the clear wall.

"On the matter of Dennis Overton."

She'd known it was coming. Once she'd made the complaint to the D.A.'s office, it was inevitable that some of the flak would scatter into her own house.

"I regret the incident, Lieutenant. However, the way it ultimately played out added to my cover rather than detracting from it."

"That's not my concern. Why didn't you report his behavior previously, to the D.A.? To me?"

They both heard the unspoken *To your father.*

"It was personal business, and until this last

incident, on my personal time. I believed I could handle it without involving my superiors or Dennis's."

He understood the defensive stance, because he understood her. "I've spoken with the district attorney. In your complaint to him you state that Overton has, over a period of time beginning the first week of April, harassed you with phone calls both here and at home, has staked out your apartment, followed you on and off duty."

"He didn't interfere with the job," she began, then wisely closed her mouth when her lieutenant stared at her.

Kiniki set aside a copy of her written statement, folded his hands on it. "Contacting you against your stated wishes when you're on duty, as well as when you're off, interferes. Are you unaware of the stalking laws, Detective?"

"No, sir. When it became apparent that the subject would not desist in his behavior, could not be discouraged and could potentially interfere with this investigation, I reported his behavior to his superior."

"You haven't filed charges."

"No, sir."

"Nor have you, as yet, requested a restraining order."

"I believe a reprimand from his superior is sufficient."

"That, or being knocked back by Jonah Blackhawk?"

She opened her mouth, closed it again. She hadn't mentioned that part of the incident to the D.A.

"Overton claims that Blackhawk attacked him, unprovoked, in a fit of jealous rage."

"Oh, for God's sake." The words, and the disgust in them, were out before she could stop them. She yanked at her hair once, then bit down on control. "That is completely inaccurate. I didn't detail the incident, Lieutenant. It didn't seem necessary. But if Dennis insists on making trouble here, I'll write out a full report."

"Do it. I want a copy on my desk by tomorrow afternoon."

"He could lose his job."

"Is that your problem?"

"No." She blew out a breath. "No, sir. Lieutenant, Dennis and I dated for a period of three months." She hated this, bringing her personal life into her superior's office. "We were… intimate, briefly. He began to display—hell."

She dropped the copspeak, approached the desk. "He got possessive, jealous, irrational. If I was late or had to cancel, he'd accuse me of being with another man. It got way out of hand, and when I broke things off he'd come by or call. Full of apologies and promises to be different. When I didn't go for it, he'd either get nasty or fall apart. Lieutenant, I slept with him. Part of this situation is my doing."

Kiniki waited a moment, pulling on his bottom lip while he studied her. "That's one of the few stupid remarks I've ever heard you make. If a victim came to you describing this situation, would you tell her it was her doing?" When she didn't answer, he nodded. "I didn't think so. You would follow procedure. Follow it now."

"Yes, sir."

"Ally…" He'd known her since she was five. He tried to keep the personal separate as religiously as she. But there were times… "Have you told your father about this?"

"I don't want to bring him into it. Respectfully, sir, I'd prefer you didn't discuss it with him."

"That's your choice. The wrong one, but yours. I'll agree to it if I have your word that if Overton so much as breathes within ten feet of you, you report it to me." He cocked his head when her lips quivered. "That's amusing?"

"No, sir. Yes." She let go of the cop to cop stand. "Jonah made nearly the same statement, Uncle Lou. I guess it's… sweet. In a manly sort of way, of course."

"Always had the smartest mouth. Go on, get out of here. And get me something on these burglaries."

Since most waitresses-in-training didn't drive classic Corvettes, Ally was in the habit of parking two blocks away and walking the rest of the distance to Blackhawk's.

It gave her time to shift gears, to appreciate what spring brought to Denver. She'd always loved the city, the way the buildings, silver towers, rode into the sky. She loved seeing the mountains go from winter-white to those steely jags laced by snow and forest.

And though she enjoyed the mountains, had spent many wonderful days in her parents' cabin, she preferred to view them from city streets. Her city.

Her city had scarred-booted cowboys walking down the same streets with Armani-clad executives. It was about cattle and commerce and nightlife. It was about the wild, coated with a sheen or polish but not quite tamed.

The east would never hold the same appeal for her.

And when spring was in full, balmy life, when the sun beamed on the white-tipped peaks that guarded Denver, when the air was thin and bright, there was no place like it in the world.

She stepped out of the city, and into Blackhawk's.

Jonah was at the bar, the far end, leaning casually, sipping what she knew was his habitual sparkling water and listening to one of his regular customers complain about his day.

Those light and beautiful green eyes pinned her the minute she walked in, stayed steady, stayed level and gave away nothing.

He hadn't touched her since the night behind the club, and had said little. It was best that way, she told herself. Mix duty and lust and you end up compromising one and being burnt by the other.

But it was frustrating to see him night after night, to remain just close enough to maintain illusions and not be able to take a complete step forward or back.

And to want him, the way she'd never wanted anyone else.

She shrugged out of her jacket and got to work.

It was killing him, by inches. Jonah knew what it was to want a woman, to have one stir blood and loins and spin images in the mind. It could be a kind of hunger that slowly churned in the belly, gnawing there until it was finally satisfied.

This was a hunger, his desire for Ally. But there was nothing of the slow churning in it. This was sharp, constant and painful.

No other woman had ever caused him pain.

He carried the taste of her inside him. He couldn't rid himself of it. That alone was infuriating. It gave her an advantage he'd never allowed another to have over him. The fact that she didn't appear to know it didn't negate the weakness.

Where you were weak, you were vulnerable.

He wanted the investigation over. He wanted her back in her own life, her own world so he could regain his balance in his.

Then he remembered the way she'd erupted against him, the way her mouth had scorched over his, and her hands fisted in his hair. And he began to worry he'd never find his feet firmly planted again.

"Good thing we don't have a cop around."

Jonah's fingers tightened on his glass, but his eyes were mild as he turned to Frannie. "What?"

She pulled a beer, poured a bump, then served it. "A guy could get arrested for looking at a woman that way. I think it's called intent or something. What you intend is pretty clear, at least when she's not looking."

"Really?" And that, he realized, was another worry. "Then I'd better watch myself."

"She's doing plenty of watching," Frannie murmured as he walked away.

"The man's got trouble on the brain," Will commented. He liked coming over to Frannie's end of the bar so he could get a whiff of her hair or maybe work a smile out of her.

"He's got woman on the brain. And he's not altogether easy with this one." She winked at him and squirted a glass of the soft drink Will drank by the gallon during working hours.

"Women never trouble the man."

"This one does."

"Well." He sipped his drink, scanned the bar crowd. "She's a looker."

"That's not it. Looks are surface stuff. This one's got him down in the gut."

"You think?" Will tugged on his little beard. He didn't understand women, and didn't pretend to. To him they were simply amazing creatures of staggering power and wonderful shapes.

"I know." She patted Will's hand and had his heart throbbing in his throat.

"Two margaritas, frozen with salt, two house drafts and a club soda with lime." Jan set down her tray and walked her fingers up Will's arm in a teasing, tickling motion. "Hey, big guy."

He blushed. He always did. "Hey, Jan. I better do a round in the club."

He hurried off and had Frannie shaking her head at Jan. "You shouldn't tease him like that."

"I can't help it. He's so sweet." She flipped her hair back. "Listen there's this party tonight. I'm going by after closing. Want to tag along?"

"After closing I'm going to be home, in my own little bed, dreaming of Brad Pitt."

"Dreaming never gets you anywhere."

"Don't I know it," Frannie muttered and sent the blender whirling.

Allison carried a full tray of empties, and had two tables worth of drink orders in the pad tucked in her bar apron. Only thirty minutes into shift, she thought. It was going to be a long night. Longer, she realized when she spotted Jonah coming toward her.

"Allison, I'd like to speak with you." About

something, anything. Five minutes alone with you might do it. Pitiful. "Would you come up to my office on your break?"

"Problem?"

"No," he lied. "No problem."

"Fine, but you'd better tell Will. He guards your cave like a wolf."

"Take your break now. Come up with me."

"Can't, thirsty people waiting. But I'll shake loose as soon as I can if it's important." She walked away quickly because she'd heard it, that underlying heat that told her what he wanted with her had nothing to do with duty.

She stopped at her station beside Pete and ordered herself to settle down. Since he was in the middle of entertaining three of the stool-sitters with a long, complicated joke, she took the time to rest her feet and study the people scattered at table and bar.

A twenty-something couple who looked like they were on the leading edge of an argument. Three suits with ties loosened arguing baseball. A flirtation, in its early stages, starting to cook between a lone woman and the better-looking of a pair of guys at the bar. Lots of eye contact and smiles.

Another couple at a table laughing together over some private joke, holding hands, she noted, flirting some even though the hands wore wedding rings. Well married, happy and financially secure if the designer handbag on the back of the woman's chair and the matching shoes were any indication.

At the next table another couple sat having a quiet conversation that seemed to please them both. There was an intimacy there as well, Ally noted. Body language, gestures, the smiling looks over sips of wine.

She envied that…comfort, she supposed, of having someone who could sit across the table in a crowded place and focus on her, care about what she said, or what she didn't have to say.

It was what her parents had—that innate rhythm and respect that added real dimension to love and attraction.

If it was lovely to watch, she wondered, how much more lovely must it be to experience?

Brooding over it, she listened to the laughter

break out at Pete's punch line. She placed her orders, listening absently to the chatter around her, scanning, always scanning the movements, the faces.

She watched the hand-holding couple signal Jan, and the woman pointing to an item on the bar menu when the waitress moved to the table to take the order. Bending down, Jan waved a hand in front of her mouth, rolled her eyes and made the woman laugh.

"The hotter the better," the woman claimed. "We don't have a club table until eight, so there's plenty of time to cool down."

When Jan had scribbled down the order and moved off, Ally found herself smiling at the way the man brought the woman's hand to his mouth and nipped at her knuckles.

If it hadn't been for that kernel of envy that kept her attention focused on them, she might have missed it. As it was, it took her several seconds to note the picture had changed.

The woman's bag still hung over the back of her chair, but at a different angle, and the outside zipper pocket wasn't quite closed.

Ally came to attention, her first thought to focus on Jan. Then she saw it. The second woman sitting with her back to the first, still smiling at her companion. While under the table, smooth and unhurried, she slipped a set of keys into the purse she held on her lap.

Bingo.

"You gone to the moon, Ally?" Pete tapped a finger on her shoulder. "I don't think anybody's waiting for vodka tonics up there."

"No, I'm right here."

As the woman rose, tucked her purse under her arm, Ally lifted her tray.

Five-four, she thought. A hundred and twenty. Brown hair, brown eyes. Late thirties with an olive complexion and strong features. And just now heading toward the ladies' room.

Rather than break cover, she hurried into the club, spotted Will and shoved the tray at him. "Sorry, table eight's waiting for these. Tell Jonah I need to speak with him. I have to do something."

"But hey."

"I have to do something," she repeated and walked briskly toward the rest rooms.

Inside, she scanned the bottom of the stalls, located the right shoes. Making a wax mold of the keys, Ally concluded and turned to one of the sinks. She ran water while she watched the shoes. It would only take a few minutes, but she'd need privacy.

Satisfied, Ally walked out.

"Ally? I got tables filling up here. Where's your tray?"

"Sorry." She shot Beth an apologetic smile. "Little emergency. I'll get on it."

She moved quickly, catching the eye of one of her team members and pausing by the table. "White female, late thirties. Brown and brown. She'll be coming out of the ladies' room in a minute. Navy jacket and slacks. She's sitting in the bar area with a white male, early forties, gray and blue in a green sweater. Keep them in sight, but don't move in. We handle it just like we outlined."

She walked back to the bar to pick up another tray as a prop. The man in the green sweater was paying the tab. Cash. He looked relaxed, but Ally noted he checked his watch and glanced back toward the rest rooms.

The woman came back in, but rather than taking her seat, stood between the tables and reached down for the short, black cape she'd draped over the chair. For a matter of seconds, her body blocked the view, then she straightened, beamed at her companion and handed him the cape.

Smart hands, Ally thought. Very smart hands.

When Jonah turned the corner of the bar, she inclined her head and let her gaze slide over to the couple preparing to leave, then back to him.

Casually she crossed over and ran a hand affectionately up and down Jonah's arm. "I've got two officers to tag them. We want them to get through the setup, all the way through. I want to give it some time before I alert the targets. When I do, I need your office."

"All right."

"We need to keep business as usual down here. If you'll hang around, I can let you know when I want to move. You can tell Beth you need me for something so she can juggle tables. I don't want any alarms going off."

"Just let me know. I'll take care of it."

"Let me have the code for your elevator. In case I need to take them up without you." She leaned in, her face tilted to his.

"Two, seven..." He leaned down, brushed his lips over hers. "Five, eight, five. Got it?"

"Yeah, I got it. See if you can keep attention off me until I move the targets out of the bar."

Her energy was up, but her mind was cool. She waited fifteen minutes. When the female target rose to use the rest room, Ally slipped in with her.

"Excuse me." After a quick check of the stalls, Ally pulled her badge out of her pocket. "I'm Detective Fletcher, Denver PD."

The woman took a quick, instinctive step in retreat. "What's this about?"

"I need your help with an investigation. I'd like to speak with you, and your husband. If you'd come with me."

"I haven't done anything."

"No, ma'am. I'll explain it all to you. There's a private office upstairs. If we could move up there as quietly as possible? I'd appreciate your cooperation."

"I'm not going anywhere without Don."

"I'll get your husband. If you'd walk back out, turn to the left, and wait in the corridor."

"I want to know what this is about."

"I'll explain it to both of you." Ally took the woman's arm to hurry her along. "Please. Just a few moments of your time."

"I don't want any trouble."

"Please wait here. I'll get your husband." Because she didn't trust the woman to stay put long, Ally moved fast. She paused at the couple's table, picked up empty glasses.

"Sir? Your wife's back there. She asked if you could come back for a minute."

"Sure. Is she okay?"

"She's fine."

Ally crossed to the bar, set down the empties. Then ducked quickly back into the corridor.

"Detective Fletcher," she said with a quick flash of her badge as the man joined her. "I need to speak with you and your wife in private." She was already keying in the code.

"She won't say what it's about. Don, I don't see why—"

"I appreciate your cooperation," Ally said again and all but shoved them both into the elevator.

"I don't appreciate being bullied by the police," the woman said with an edge of nerves in her voice.

"Lynn, calm down. It's okay."

"I'm sorry to be abrupt." Ally stepped into Jonah's office, gestured to the chairs. "If you'd have a seat, I'll fill you in."

Lynn crossed her arms, hugged her elbows tight. "I don't want to sit down."

Have it your way, sister, Ally thought. "I'm investigating a series of burglaries in and around Denver during the last several weeks."

The woman sniffed. "Do we look like burglars?"

"No, ma'am. You look like a nice, well-established, upper class couple. Which has been, to date, the main target of this burglary ring. And less than twenty minutes ago, a woman we suspect is part of that ring lifted your keys out of your purse."

"That's impossible. My purse has been right with me all night." As if to prove it, she started to unzip the pocket. Ally snagged her wrist.

"Please don't touch your keys."

"How can I touch them if they're not there?" the woman argued.

"Lynn, shut up. Come on." He squeezed his wife's shoulder. "What's going on?" he asked Ally.

"We believe molds are made of the keys. They're replaced and the targeted victim remains unaware. Then their house is broken into and their belongings are stolen. We'd like to prevent that from happening to you. Now sit down."

Authority snapped in her voice this time. Visibly shaken, the woman lowered herself into a chair.

"If I could have your names please."

"Don and Lynn—Mr. and Mrs. Barnes."

"Mr. Barnes, would you give me your address?"

He swallowed, sat on the arm of his wife's chair and rattled it off while Ally noted it down. "Do you mean someone's in our house right now? Robbing us right now?"

"I don't believe they can move quite that quickly." In her mind she was calculating the drive-time. "Is there anyone at that address right now?"

"No. It's just us. Man." Barnes ran a hand through his hair. "Man, this is weird."

"I'm going to call in your address and begin setting up a stakeout. Give me a second."

She picked up the phone as the elevator doors opened, and Jonah walked it. "I've got it covered here," she told him.

"I'm sure you do. Mr. and Mrs…?"

"Barnes," the man answered. "Don and Lynn Barnes."

"Don, can I offer you and your wife something to drink? I realize this is very inconvenient and upsetting for you."

"I could use a shot. A good stiff bourbon, I think."

"Can't blame you. And Lynn?"

"I…" She lifted a hand, dropped it. "I just can't…I don't understand."

"Maybe a little brandy." Jonah turned away, opened a panel in the wall to reveal a small, well-stocked bar. "You can put yourselves in Detective Fletcher's capable hands," he continued and he chose bottles and glasses. "And meanwhile, we'll try to keep you as comfortable as possible."

"Thanks." Lynn took the brandy from him. "Thank you so much."

"Mr. Barnes." A little miffed at how smoothly Jonah had settled ruffled feathers, she yanked the man's attention back to her. "We have units on the way to your house right now. Can you describe your house for me? The layout, doors, windows?

"Sure." He laughed, a little shakily. "Hell, I'm an architect."

He gave her a clear picture, which she relayed to the team before she began to set up the coordinates for the stakeout.

"You have dinner reservations here tonight?" Ally asked them.

"Yeah. Eight o'clock. We're making a night of it," he said with a sour smile.

Ally checked her watch. "They'll think they have plenty of time." She wanted them to go back down, to finish their time at the bar, go into dinner and present the appearance of normality. And one look at the woman's face told her it was a long shot.

"Mrs. Barnes. Lynn." Ally came back around the desk, sat on the edge of it. "We're going to stop these people. They won't take your things or damage your home. But I need you to help me out here. I need you and your husband to go back down, to try to get through the evening as if nothing was wrong. If you could hold on for another hour, I think we could wrap this up."

"I want to go home."

"We'll get you there. Give me an hour. It's possible that a member of the organization is assigned to keep an eye on you. You've already been away from your table nearly twenty minutes. We'll cover that, but we can't cover another hour. We don't want to scare these people off."

"If they're scared off, they won't break into my house."

"No, just into someone else's the next time."

"Give me a minute with her, okay." Barnes got up, took his wife's hands. "Come on, Lynn. Hell, it's an adventure. We'll eat out on the story for years. Come on, let's go—let's just go downstairs and get drunk."

"Jonah, go with them. Ah, pass the word that those—what was it—the wild wings you ordered didn't sit too well after all. You're fine now, but you were feeling a little sick. Blackhawk's will cover your bar bill, right?"

"Naturally." Jonah offered Lynn his hand to help her to her feet. "And the dinner tab. I'll take you down. You just needed to stretch out for a few minutes, and I offered to take you and your husband up to my office until you felt better. Good enough?" he asked Ally as he pressed for the elevator.

"Perfect. I need to make a couple more calls, then I'll be down. I'm going to have to cut out before end of shift. I've had a family emergency."

"Good luck with it," he told her, and led the Barneses away.

Chapter 6

She got the key from Jonah and went straight to the employee lounge for her bag. She ran straight out, doing no more than waving a hand when Frannie called out to her from behind the bar.

She was trusting Jonah to answer any questions. No one could do it better, she thought as she raced the blocks to her car. A simple word, a shrug from him and that would be that. No one pumped a man like Jonah Blackhawk.

She had to get to Federal Heights before everything went down.

At first she thought she was seeing things. But the night was clear and cool and her vision excellent. There was no mistaking the fact that all four of her tires were slashed.

She swore, kicked viciously at the mangled rubber. A hell of a time, she thought, one hell of a time for Dennis Overton to get nasty. Digging into her bag she pulled out her cell phone and called for a radio car.

Time wasted, was all she could think. Two minutes, five minutes ticking away while she paced the sidewalk and waited. She had her badge out and her teeth clenched when the patrol car pulled up.

"Got some trouble, Detective?"

"Yeah. Hit the sirens, head north on 25. I'll tell you when to go silent."

"You got it. What's going down?"

She settled into the back behind the two uniforms, itching to have her hands on the wheel and her foot on the gas. "I'll fill you in." She took her weapon and harness out of her bag, and felt more herself the minute she strapped it on.

"Call for a tow truck, will you? I don't want to leave my car on the street like that."

"Shame about that. Nice car."

"Yeah." She forgot about it as they screamed up the interstate.

A block from the Barneses' address, she hopped out of the car, and arrowed straight to Hickman. "Give me the story."

"They took their time getting here. Balou and Dietz had the first leg of the tail and said they drove like solid citizens, kept under the speed limit, signaled for turns. Woman riding shotgun, made a call on a cell phone. He turned over the tail to me and Carson when they got on 36. They stopped for gas. The woman gets in the back. They're driving a nice, suburban minivan. She's doing something back there, but I couldn't get close enough to see."

"Making the keys. I bet you two weeks' pay she's got the works for it in the van."

"Do I look like I take sucker bets?" He glanced down the quiet street. "Anyhow, we had a unit here, waiting. The suspects were observed parking the van a block down from the target address. They strolled up the street, walked right up to the door, unlocked it and went in like they owned the place."

"Barnes said they have a security system."

"Alarm didn't trip. They've been inside about ten minutes now. Lieutenant's waiting for you. We've got the area blocked off, the house surrounded."

"Then let's move in and wrap this up."

He grinned, handed her a walkie-talkie. "Saddle up."

"God, I love cowboy talk."

They moved fast, kept low. She spotted the cops positioned on the street, behind trees, in shadows, hunched in cars.

"Glad you could join the party, Detective." Kiniki nodded toward the house. "Ballsy, aren't they?"

Lights gleamed, a homey glow against windows on the first and second floor. While Ally watched, she saw a faint shadow move behind the lower window.

"Dietz and Balou are covering the back. We've got them closed in. What's your play?"

Ally reached in her pocket, pulled out keys. "We move in on all sides, and go in the front. When we move, pull one of the radio cars across the driveway. Let's block that route."

"Call it."

She lifted the walkie-talkie, to establish positioning and give the orders. And all hell broke loose.

Three gunshots blasted the air, the return fire slamming into the echoes. Even as Ally drew her own weapon, voices shouted through the walkie-talkies.

"Dietz is down! Officer down! Shooter's male, heading east on foot. Officer down!"

Cops rushed the house. Ally hit the door first, went in low. Blood pounded in her ears as she swept the area with her weapon. Hickman took her back, and at her signal headed up the stairs while she turned right.

Someone was shouting. She heard it like a buzz in the brain. Lights flashed on.

The house opened out like a fan. She brought

the layout Barnes had described into her mind as she and the rest of the team spread out. At each doorway she led with eyes and weapon, following training while her breath came short and shallow.

There was more gunfire from outside, muffled pops. She started to turn in that direction and saw the sliding door on what looked like a small solarium wasn't quite shut.

She caught a scent, very female, and following instinct turned away from the shouts and bolted for the door.

She saw the woman, just the silhouette of her, running hard toward a line of ornamental trees. "Police! Stop where you are!"

She would replay it a dozen times. The woman continued to run. Weapon drawn, Ally raced after her, calling out the warning, shouting her position and situation into her hand unit.

She heard calls from behind her, running feet.

They'd cut her off, Ally thought. Cut her off even before she reached the six foot fence that closed in the property.

Nowhere to go.

She gained ground, caught both the scent of

perfume and panic sweat the woman left on the air. Moonlight picked her out of the shadows, the swing of her dark hair, the stream of the short, black cape.

And when, on the run, the woman turned, the moonlight bounced off the chrome plating of the revolver in her hand.

Ally saw her lift it, felt with a kind of detached shock the heat of the bullet that whined past her own head.

"Drop your weapon! Drop it now!"

And as the woman pivoted, and the gun jerked in her hand, Ally fired.

Ally saw the woman stagger, heard the thud as the gun fell from her hand, and heard a kind of sighing gasp. But what she would remember, what seemed to burn on her brain like acid on glass, was the dark stain that bloomed between the woman's breasts even as she dropped.

It was bone-deep training that had her rushing forward, stepping on the woman's gun. "Suspect down," she said into her hand unit as she crouched to check for a pulse. Her voice didn't shake, and neither did she. Not yet.

It was Hickman who got to her first. She

heard his voice like something carried on the crest of a wave of churning water. Her head was full of sound, a rushing liquid sound.

"Are you hit? Ally, are you hit?"

His hands were already moving over her, tugging at her jacket to check for injury.

"Call an ambulance." Her lips were stiff, they felt wooden, splintered. She reached forward, crossing her hands over each other, pressing the heels of them on the woman's chest.

"On the way. Come on. Get up."

"She needs pressure on this wound. She needs an ambulance."

"Ally." He holstered his own weapon. "You can't do anything for her. She's dead."

She didn't let herself be sick. She made herself stand and watch as the wounded officer and the woman's partner were loaded into ambulances. She made herself watch when the woman was zipped into a thick black bag.

"Detective Fletcher."

And she made herself turn, face her lieutenant. "Sir. Can you tell me Dietz's condition?"

"I'm on my way to the hospital. We'll know more later."

She rubbed the back of her hand over her mouth. "The suspect?"

"Paramedics said he'll make it. It'll be a couple of hours at least before we can question him."

"Am I...will I be allowed to be in on the interrogation."

"It's still your case." He took her arm to draw her away. "Ally, listen to me. I know what it feels like. Ask yourself now, right now, if you could have done anything differently."

"I don't know."

"Hickman was behind you, and Carson was coming in from the left. I haven't spoken with her as yet, but Hickman's report is you identified yourself, ordered her to stop. She turned and fired. You ordered her to drop her weapon, and she prepared to fire again. You had no choice. That's what I expect to hear from you during the standard inquiry tomorrow morning. Do you want me to call your father?"

"No. Please. I'll talk to him tomorrow, after the inquiry."

"Then go home, get some rest. I'll let you know about Dietz."

"Sir, unless I'm relieved of duty, I'd rather go to the hospital. Stand by for Dietz, and be on hand to question the suspect when we're cleared to do so."

It would be better for her, he thought, to do what came next. "You can ride with me."

Panic was like an animal clawing at his throat. He'd never felt anything like it before. Jonah told himself it was just hospitals that did it to him. He'd always detested them. The smell of them brought back the last hideous months of his father's life, and made him all too aware that a turn here, a turn there in a different direction might have damned him to experience the same fate his father had at fifty years old.

His source had assured him that Ally wasn't hurt. But all he knew for certain was that something had gone very wrong at the bust and she was at the hospital. That had been enough to have him heading straight out. Just to see for himself, he thought.

He found her, slumped in a chair, in the hallway of Intensive Care. The panic digging into his throat released.

She'd taken the clip out of her hair as he knew she did when she was tense or tired. The gilt curtain of hair fanned down the side of her face, concealing it. But the tired slouch, the hands she gripped together on her knees, told him what to expect.

He stepped in front of her, crouched down and saw, as he'd known he would, pale skin and dark, bruised eyes.

"Hey." He gave in to the need to lay his hand over hers. "Bad day?"

"Pretty bad." It seemed like wires were crossed in her brain. She didn't think to wonder why he was there. "One of my team's in critical condition. They don't know if he'll make it till morning."

"I'm sorry."

"Yeah, me, too. The doctors won't let us talk to the son of a bitch who shot him. Male suspect identified as Richard Fricks. He's sleeping comfortably under a nice haze of drugs while Dietz fights for his life, and his wife's down in the chapel praying for it."

She wanted to close her eyes, to go into the dark, but kept them open and on his. "And for a bonus, I killed a woman tonight. One shot through the heart. Like she was a target I aced at practice."

Her hands trembled once under his, then fisted.

"Yeah, that's a pretty bad day. Come on."

"Come where?"

"Home, I'm taking you home." When she looked at him blankly, he pulled her to her feet. She felt featherlight, her hands fragile as glass. "There's nothing you can do here now, Ally."

She closed her eyes, groped for a breath. "That's what Hickman said at the scene. There's nothing you can do. Looks like you're both right."

She let him lead her to the elevator. There was no point in staying, or arguing or pretending she wanted to be alone. "I can...get a ride."

"You've got one."

No, she thought, no point in arguing, or in resisting the supporting arm he slipped around her waist. "How did you know to come here?"

"A cop came by to take the Barneses home. I

got enough out of him to know there'd been
trouble, and where you were. Why isn't your
father with you?"

"He doesn't know. I'll tell him about it
tomorrow."

"What the hell's wrong with you?"

She blinked, like a woman coming out of a
dark room into the light. "What?"

He pulled her out of the elevator, across the
hospital lobby. "Do you want him to hear about
this from someone else? To not hear your voice,
hear you tell him you're not hurt? What are you
thinking?"

"I…I wasn't thinking. You're right." She
fumbled in her purse for her phone as they crossed
the lot. "I need a minute. I just need a minute."

She got into the car, steadying herself, steadying her breathing. "Okay," she whispered it to
herself as Jonah started the car. She punched in
the number, waited through the first ring, then
heard her mother's voice.

"Mom." Her breath hitched. She bore down,
holding a hand over the phone until she was sure
her voice would be normal. "I'm fine. Every-

thing okay there? Uh-huh. Listen, I'm on my way home, and I need to speak to Dad a minute. Yeah, that's right. Cop talk. Thanks."

Now she closed her eyes, listened to her mother call out, heard the warm mix of their laughter before her father's voice sounded in her ear.

"Ally? What's up?"

"Dad." Her voice wanted to crack but she refused to let it. "Don't say anything to upset Mom."

There was a pause. "All right."

"I'm okay. I'm not hurt, and I'm on my way home. It went down tonight, and things went wrong. Ah, one of the team was wounded, and he's in the hospital. One of the suspects is in there, too. We'll know more tomorrow on both."

"You're all right? Allison?"

"Yes, I wasn't hurt. Dad. Dad, I had to fire my weapon. They were armed. Both suspects were armed and opened fire. She wouldn't…I killed her."

"I'll be there in ten minutes."

"No, please. Stay with Mom. You'll have to tell her and she's going to be upset. I need to…I just need to go home and—tomorrow, okay? Can we talk about it tomorrow? I'm so tired now."

"If that's what you want."

"It is. I promise, I'm all right."

"Ally, who went down?"

"Dietz. Len Dietz." She lifted her free hand, pressed her fingers to her lips. They didn't feel stiff now, but soft. Painfully soft. "He's critical. The lieutenant's still at the hospital."

"I'll contact him. Try to get some sleep. But you call, anytime, if you change your mind. I can be there. We both can."

"I know. I'll call you in the morning. I think it'll be easier in the morning. I love you."

She broke the connection, let the phone slide into her purse. She opened her eyes and saw they were already in front of her apartment. "Thanks for…"

Jonah said nothing, simply got out, came around to her door. Opening it, he held out a hand for hers. "I can't seem to get my thoughts lined up. What time is it?"

"It doesn't matter. Give me your key."

"Oh, yeah, the traditionalist." She dug it

out, unaware her other hand was clutching his like a lifeline. "I'm going to start expecting flowers next."

She walked through the lobby, to the elevator. "It seems like there's something I have to do. I can't get a rope around what it is, though. There should be something I have to do. We identified her. She had ID anyway. Madeline Fricks. Madeline Ellen Fricks," she murmured, floating like a dream out of the elevator. "Age thirty-seven. She had an address in…Englewood. Somebody's checking it out. I should be checking it out."

He unlocked the door, drew her inside. "Sit down, Ally."

"Yeah, I could sit down." She looked blankly around the living room. It was just the way she'd left it that morning. Nothing had changed. Why did it seem as if everything had changed?

Jonah solved the matter by picking her up and carrying her toward the bedroom.

"Where are we going?"

"You're going to lie down. Got anything to drink around here?"

"Stuff."

"Fine. I'll go find some stuff." He laid her on the bed.

"I'll be okay."

"That's right." He left her to hunt through the kitchen. In a narrow cupboard he found an unopened bottle of brandy. He broke the seal, poured three fingers. When he brought it back, she was sitting up in the bed, her knees rammed into her chest, her arms roped around them.

"I've got the shakes." She kept her face pressed to her knees. "If I had something to do, I wouldn't have the shakes."

"Here's what you need to do." He sat on the bed, cupped a hand under her chin and lifted it. "Drink this."

She took the first sip obediently when he lifted the glass to her lips. Then she coughed and turned her head away. "I hate brandy. Somebody gave me that last Christmas, God knows why. I meant to…" She trailed off, began to rock.

"Have some more. Come on, Fletcher, take your medicine."

He gave her little choice but to gulp down another swallow. Her eyes watered and color flooded her cheeks. "We had the place closed in, surrounded the house, cordoned off the area in a three-block radius. They couldn't have gotten through. They had no place to run."

She needed to talk through it. Jonah set the brandy aside. "But they ran anyway."

"We were just about to move in, and he— Fricks—came out the back, already firing. He hit Dietz with two rounds. Some of us went around the back, covering both sides. Some of us went in the front. I was first in, Hickman was behind me. We spread out, started the sweep."

She could still see it in her head. Moving through, fast and steady, the lights blazing.

"I could hear more gunfire, and shouting from outside. I nearly turned back, thinking they were both out of the house and running—that they were together. But I saw—there's this bump-out sunroom deal on the house, and the sliding door leading out wasn't closed, not all the way closed. I spotted her as soon as I stepped out. Going in the opposite direction as her partner. Splitting us up, I guess. I called out, told her to stop. I was in pursuit and she fired a round. Sloppy shot. I ordered her to stop, to drop her weapon. I didn't see she had a choice. Where the hell could she go? But she spun around.

"She spun around," Ally repeated. "The moon was very bright, very bright and it was on her face, in her eyes, shining on the gun. And I shot her."

"Did you have a choice?"

Her lips trembled open. "No. In my head that's clear. Jonah, that's so clear. I've gone over it, step after step, a dozen times already. But they don't prepare you for what it's like. They can't. They can't tell you how it feels."

The first tear spilled over and she wiped it impatiently away. "I don't even know what I'm crying for. Or who."

"It doesn't matter." He put his arms around her, drew her head down on his shoulder and held her while she wept.

And while she wept he went back over what she'd told him.

Sloppy shot, she'd said, almost skimming over the fact that someone had tried to kill her. Yet she wept because she'd had no choice but to take a life.

Cops. He turned his cheek against her hair. He'd never understand cops.

She slept for two hours, dropping into oblivion like a stone in a pool, and staying deep at the bottom. When she woke, she was wrapped around him in the dark.

She lay still a moment, orienting herself, while his heart beat strong and steady under her palm. With her eyes open and her mind clearing she went through a mental check list. She had a vague headache, but nothing major—just a hangover from the crying jag. There was a stronger feeling of embarrassment, but she thought she could live with that, too.

She wiggled her toes and discovered she was barefoot. And her ankle holster was gone.

So, she realized, was her shoulder harness.

He'd disarmed her, she thought, in more ways than one. She'd blubbered out her story, cried on his shoulder and was now wrapped around him in the dark. Worse than all of that was realizing she wanted to stay there.

Believing him asleep she started to inch away.

"Feel any better?"

She didn't jolt, but it was close. "Yeah. Considerably. I guess I owe you."

"I guess you do."

In the dark he found her mouth with his and sank in.

Soft, unexpectedly soft. Warm, deliciously warm. Yes, she wanted to stay there, and so she opened for him, sliding her hand from his heart to his face, yielding when he turned his body to press hers into the mattress.

The good solid weight of him, the hard lines of his body, the drugging heat of his mouth was exactly what she wanted. Her arms came around him, holding him there as he had held her in tears and in sleep.

He gave himself the moment, the dark taste of her mouth, the sleepy sigh she made, the feminine give of her beneath him. He'd lain beside her, his body alert, his mind restless while hers slept. Wanting her, wanting her so it was like a fever in the blood.

Yet when she woke, he found himself drowning in tenderness.

Yet when she surrendered, he found himself unwilling, unable, to take.

He drew back, skimmed a thumb over the curve of her cheek. "Bad timing," he said and rolled off the bed.

"I…" She cleared her throat. Her body had just started to ache, her mind had just started to float. Now she floundered free. "Look, if you have some weird idea that you were taking advantage, you're wrong."

"Am I?"

"I know how to say yes or no. And while I appreciate you bringing me home, hearing me out and not leaving me alone, I'm not grateful enough for any of that to pay you back with sex. I think too much of myself. Hell, I think too much of sex."

He laughed, sat on the edge of the bed again. "You do feel better."

"I said I did. So." She slid over, tossing her hair back and nuzzling his throat.

His pulse tripped and a fireball burst in his belly. "That's tempting." He was lucky to be able to breathe, and still casually patted her hand and got to his feet. "But no thanks."

Insult came first, and something vile nearly spilled off her tongue. Because it made her think of Dennis, she yanked herself back. "Okay. Mind if I ask why? Under the current circumstances, that seems like a reasonable question."

"Two reasons."

He switched on the bedside light, watched her eyes narrow in defense. And the look of her slammed into him like a fist in the throat.

"God. You're beautiful."

A little thrill jumped up her spine. "And that's why you don't want to make love with me?"

"I want you. Enough that it's starting to hurt. That ticks me off."

Idly he took the ends of her hair, wrapped a length of it around his hand, released it. "You're on my mind, Ally, too often for comfort. I like to be comfortable. So reason one is that I haven't decided if I want to get tangled up with you. If I do half of the very interesting things I have in mind to do with you, I'm going to be tangled."

She sat back on her heels. "I imagine you know how to cut line when you want to."

"I've never had any trouble before. You're trouble. It's that simple."

Insult and annoyance had vanished. "This is fascinating. Here I had you pegged as somebody who took what he wanted when he wanted it, and the hell with the consequences."

"No. I prefer calculating, then eliminating consequences. Then I take what I want."

"In other words, I make you nervous."

"Oh, yeah. Go ahead and grin," he said with a nod. "I can't blame you."

She laughed, lifted her eyebrows. "You said there were two reasons. What's the second?"

"That's easy." He stepped to the bed, bent down and caught her chin in his hand. "I don't like cops," he said, and brushed his lips lightly over hers.

When he would have leaned away from the kiss, she leaned in, sliding up so that her body rubbed over his. She felt his body quiver, and nothing had ever been more satisfying.

"Yeah, you're trouble," he muttered. "I'm leaving."

"Coward."

"Okay, that stings, but I'll get over it." He

walked over to shrug on the jacket he'd tossed onto a chair, slip his feet back into his shoes.

She didn't just feel better, Ally realized. She felt fabulous. Invincible. "Why don't you come on back here and fight like a man."

He glanced at her. She knelt on the side of the bed, her eyes dark and challenging, her hair a tumble of gold around her face and shoulders.

The taste of her was still sizzling on his tongue.

But he shook his head, walked to the door. Tormented himself with one last look. "I'm going to hate both of us in the morning," he told her, then strode away while her laughter followed him.

Chapter 7

Ally was up at six and ready to roll out the door at seven. She nearly rolled right over her parents, who were at her front door.

"Mom." She flicked her eyes up to her father, started to speak, but her mother already had her caught in a hard hug. "Mom," she said again. "I'm all right."

"Indulge me." Cilla held on, tight, heart pressed to heart, cheek pressed to cheek.

Stupid, Cilla thought, so stupid to have kept

it together all night and to feel herself falling apart now that her child was in her arms.

She couldn't, wouldn't allow it.

"Okay." She laid her lips on Ally's temple for a moment, then drew back far enough to study her daughter's face.

"I had to see for myself. You're lucky your father held me off this long."

"I didn't want you to worry."

"It's my job to worry. And I believe in doing a job well."

Ally watched her mother's lips curve, saw the tears willed away. And knew it cost her. "You do everything well."

Cilla O'Roarke Fletcher's eyes were the same golden-brown as her daughter's, her short sweep of hair a luxuriant black that suited her angular features and smoky voice.

"But I've got worry down to a science," she said.

Since they were almost of identical heights, Ally had only to shift closer to kiss Cilla's cheek. "Well, you can take a break. I'm fine. Really."

"I suppose you look it."

"Come on inside. I can make some more coffee."

"No, you're on your way out. I just needed to see you." To touch you, Cilla thought. My baby. "I'm heading into work. I'm interviewing a new sales manager at KHIP. Your dad's dropping me off. You can use my car today."

"How did you know I needed a car?"

"I have connections," Boyd told her. "You should have yours back by midafternoon."

"I would've handled it." Ally shut the door behind her, frowned.

"Meaning you would have handled the car, and Overton and the tangle of bureaucracy," Cilla put in. "I hope I didn't raise a daughter who's ungrateful, and who expects her father to stand back with his hands in his pockets when something happens to her." Cilla tilted her head, lifted her brows. "I'd be very disappointed if I had."

Boyd grinned, slipped an arm around Cilla's shoulders and pressed his lips to her hair.

"Good one," Ally muttered, properly chastised. "Thank you, Dad."

"You're welcome, Allison."

"Now, which one of us is going to go beat the tar out of Dennis Overton?" Cilla rubbed her hands together. "Or can we all do it? In which case, I get to go first."

"She has violent tendencies," Ally pointed out.

"Tell me about it. Down girl," he told Cilla. "Let the system work. Now…Detective." Boyd draped his arm around his daughter's shoulders as they walked to the elevator. "You're to report to the hospital first. There's a suspect who needs to be questioned."

"The inquiry into the shooting?"

"Will proceed this morning. You'll need to give your statement and file your report. By ten hundred. Detective Hickman filed his last night, which gives a very clear picture. You don't have anything to worry about."

"I'm not worried. I know I did what I had to do. It gave me some bad moments last night." She blew out a breath. "Some pretty bad ones. But I'm okay with it now. As okay as it gets, I guess."

"You shouldn't have been alone last night," Cilla said.

"Actually I had…a friend with me for a while."

Boyd opened his mouth, shut it again. After Ally's call the night before, he'd contacted Kiniki immediately. He knew that Jonah had driven Ally home from the hospital, so he had a good idea just who the friend was.

But he had no idea how he felt about it.

Ally pulled in to the hospital visitors' lot, circled until she found a space. She spotted Hickman as she set the locks and alarm.

"Nice ride," he commented, hands in pockets, eyes squinted into slits against the brilliant sunshine. "Not every cop's got herself a Mercedes as a backup vehicle."

"It's my mother's."

"You've got some mother." He'd seen Cilla, so he knew it was true. "So, how's it going?"

"Okay." She fell into step beside him. "Look, I know you already filed your report on last night's incident. I appreciate you getting it in so fast, and backing me up."

"It happened the way it happened. If it smoothes any edges for you, you should know that you fired about a split hair before I did. If

I'd been in the lead instead of you, I'd've been the one to take her out."

"Thanks. Any word on Dietz?"

"Still critical." Hickman's expression darkened. "He made it through the night, so that's hopeful. I want a round with the son of a bitch who put him here."

"Get in line."

"You know how you want to play it?"

"I've been thinking about it." They moved together across the lobby to the bank of elevators. "She made a call from her cell phone; that puts at least one other person in on the deal. I say two. Whoever's inside the club, and somebody pushing the buttons, organizing. Our guy here shot a cop, so he knows he's going down hard. His wife's dead, his operation's broken and he's looking at Death Row."

"Doesn't give him much incentive to talk. You going to deal him a life sentence?"

"That's the road. Let's make sure he walks it."

She showed her badge to the uniform on guard at Fricks's door, walked through.

Fricks lay in bed, his skin pale, slightly gray.

His eyes were blurred, but open. His gaze passed over Ally and Hickman, then returned to contemplate the ceiling.

"I have nothing to say. I want a lawyer."

"Well, that makes our job easier." Hickman walked over to the bed, pursed his lips. "Doesn't look like a cop killer, does he, Fletcher?"

"He's not. Yet. Dietz might make it. Of course, this guy here's still looking at being strapped to a table and being put down like a sick dog. Nighttime B and E, burglary, possession of an unregistered weapon, assault with a deadly, attempted murder of a police officer." She moved her shoulders. "And plenty more where that came from."

"I have nothing to say."

"Then shut up," she suggested. "Why try to help yourself? Trust a lawyer to take care of everything. But…I'm not in the mood to make deals with lawyers. How about you, Hickman?"

"Nope, can't say that's my mood at this time."

"We're not in the mood," Ally repeated. "Not when we have a fellow officer fighting for his life up in Intensive Care. That really puts us off lawyers who look for ways to wiggle cop killers out of the noose. Right, Hickman?"

"Yeah, puts me right off. I don't see any reason we should give this guy any kind of a break. I say let him hang for it all by himself."

"Well, we ought to look at the big picture, though. Show a little compassion. He lost his wife last night." She watched the ripple of pain run over Fricks's face before he closed his eyes.

There, she thought, was the key to him.

"That's rough. His wife's dead, and he's lying here shot up and looking at a death sentence." Ally lifted her shoulders, let them fall. "Maybe he's not thinking how other people, people who helped put him in this situation could walk away clean. Clean, and rich, while he's twisting in the wind on a very short rope. And his wife gets put in the ground."

She leaned over the bed. "But he ought to be thinking about it. Of course maybe he didn't love his wife."

"Don't talk to me about Madeline." His voice wavered. "She was my heart."

"Really. I'm touched. That touches me. Now

that might not hold any weight with Hickman here, but me, I've got a soft spot for true love. Since I do, I'm going to tell you you ought to be thinking how you can help yourself now, because if you were her heart, she wouldn't want you to go down for this alone."

His eyes flickered, then closed.

"You ought to be thinking that if you cooperate and tell us what we want to know, we'll go to the D.A. and press for a little leniency. Show some remorse now, Richard, reach out. That'll go a long way toward keeping you off a table in a little room a few years down the road."

"I talk, I'm already dead."

Ally shot Hickman a glance. "You'll get protection."

Fricks's eyes were still closed, but tears began to leak out of them. "I loved my wife."

"I know you did." Ally lowered the bed guard so she could sit beside him.

Intimacy now, she thought. Sympathy. And infused her voice with both. "I saw you together at Blackhawk's. The way you looked at each other tells me you had something special between you."

"She—she's gone."

"But you tried to save her, didn't you, Richard? You ran out of the house first, to cover for her. That's why you're in this jam. She loved you. She'd want you to help yourself. She'd want you to go on living, to do whatever you had to do to go on. Richard, you tried to save her last night, drawing the cops off her so she could get away. You did what you could. Now you've got to save yourself."

"No one was supposed to get hurt. The guns were just a precaution, to scare anybody off if something went wrong."

"That's right. You didn't plan on this. I believe that. That'll make a difference how this all comes out for you. Things just got out of control."

"Nothing ever went wrong before. She panicked. That's all. She just panicked, and I couldn't think of anything else to do."

"You didn't mean to hurt anybody." Ally kept her voice quiet, compassionate, even while the image of Dietz, bleeding on the ground, ran through her mind. "You just wanted to give her time to get away." She took a moment while he wept.

"How'd you get past the alarm systems?"

"I've got a knack for electronics." He took the tissues she handed him, wiped his eyes. "I worked in security. People don't always remember to set their alarms anyway. But when they did, I could usually disarm them. If I couldn't, it was a wash and we walked away. Where have they put Madeline? Where is she?"

"We'll talk about that. Help me out here, and I'll do what I can to arrange for you to see her. Who called you from the club, Richard, to tell you something was wrong with the Barneses? Was it the same person Madeline called from the car?"

He let out a sobbing breath, shook his head. "I want immunity."

Hickman let out a snort, made a move to draw Ally off the bed, make her the protector. "The son of a bitch wants immunity. You're bending over backward to help him out, and he wants a walk. Screw him. Let him hang."

"Hold on. Just hold on. Can't you see the

man's upset? Lying here like this, he can't even make arrangements for his wife's funeral."

"She—" Fricks turned his head away, and his chest heaved once. "She wanted to be cremated. It was important to her."

"We can help you arrange that. We can help you give her what she wanted. You have to give us something back."

"Immunity."

"Listen, Richard. You can't ask for the moon and stars on this one. Now I could make you promises, but I'm being straight with you. Best I can do is leniency."

"We don't need him, Ally." Hickman picked up the chart at the foot of the bed, scanned it. "We got him cold, and we'll pick up the rest of the pieces within a couple of days."

"He's right." Ally let out a sigh, looked back at Fricks. "A couple of days, maybe less, we'll have all the answers. But if you save us some time, some trouble, prove you're remorseful over shooting that cop, I can promise to go to bat for you. We know there are other people involved. It's just a matter of time before we get to them.

Help me out, I'll help you. I'll help you do what you need to do for Madeline. That's fair."

"It was her brother." He said it between his teeth, then opened his eyes. They were no longer blurry, no longer wet, but burning dry with hate. "He talked her into it. He could talk her into anything. It was going to be an adventure, exciting. He set it up, all of it. He's the reason she's dead."

"Where is he?"

"He has a house down in Littleton. Big house on the lake. His name's Matthew Lyle, and he'll be coming after me for what happened to Madeline. He's crazy. I tell you he's crazy, and he's obsessed with her. He'll kill me."

"Okay, don't worry. He won't get near you." Ally took out her notebook. "Tell me more about Matthew Lyle."

At four that afternoon, Jonah was settled behind his desk, trying to work. He was furious with himself for calling Ally three times, twice at home, once at the station. And equally furious she'd made no attempt to get back to him.

He'd decided he'd made a very big mistake by walking out of her apartment instead of staying with her in the dark, in the bed, instead of taking what he wanted.

It was a mistake he'd have to live with, and he was certain he could live with it more comfortably than live with the options.

All he wanted now was the simple courtesy of information. Damn it, she owed him that. He'd let her into his life, into his business, let her work side by side with his friends while she deceived them. While he deceived them.

Now, by God, he wanted answers.

He snatched the phone up again just as the elevator doors slid open. And Ally walked through.

"I still had your code."

Saying nothing, he replaced the receiver. She was dressed for work, he noted. Cop work. "I'll make a note to have it changed."

Her eyebrows rose but she continued across the room and dropped comfortably into the chair across from his desk. "I figured you'd want an update."

"You figured correctly."

Something was in his craw, she noted. They'd get to that later. "Fricks rolled over on his brother-in-law. Matthew Lyle, aka Lyle Matthews, aka Lyle Delaney. Computer crimes mostly, with some assaults. He's got a long sheet, but most of the charges were dumped. Insufficient evidence, deals. Did some psych time, though. He's cleared out. We hit his place a couple of hours ago, and he's gone."

She paused long enough to rub her eyes. "Didn't have time to take everything with him. The house was packed with stolen goods. From what it looks like they've turned very little, if anything. Place looked like an auction house. Oh, and you're going to be short a waitress tonight."

"I didn't think you'd be reporting for work tonight."

"No, I didn't mean me. Jan. According to Fricks, she and Lyle are…" She lifted a hand, crossed two fingers. "Very close. She's the inside man. Scanned for the marks, passed the credit card number to Lyle via beeper. The Fricks move in, she helps cover for them while they lift the keys. Then she alerts them with another code when the targets call for their check. Gives the Fricks time to finish up, clear out. Very smooth all in all."

"Have you got her?"

"No, doesn't look like she went home last night. My guess is she went straight to Lyle, and they went under together. We will get her. We'll get them both."

"I don't doubt it. I suppose that ends your association with Blackhawk's."

"Looks like." She rose, wandered to the window. He had the blinds shut today, so she tapped a slat up, looked out. "I'll need to interview your people. I thought they'd feel more comfortable if I did it here. Do you have any problem with me using your office for it?"

"No."

"Great. I'll start with you. Get it out of the way." She came back to sit, took out her notepad. "Tell me what you know about Jan."

"She's worked here about a year. She was good at her job, a favorite with a number of the regulars. Had a knack for remembering names. She was reliable and efficient."

"Did you have a personal relationship with her?"

"No."

"But you're aware she lives in the same apartment building as Frannie?"

"Is that against the law?"

"How did you come to hire her?"

"She applied for the job. Frannie has nothing to do with this."

"I didn't say she did." Ally took a photo out of her bag. "Have you ever seen this man in here?"

Jonah glanced at the police photo of a dark-haired man of about thirty. "No."

"See him anywhere else?"

"No. Is this Lyle?"

"That's right. Why are you angry with me?"

"Irritated," he corrected coolly. "I'd classify it as irritated. I don't care to be interrogated by the police."

"I'm a cop, Jonah. That's a fact." She put the photo back into her bag. "I've got a job to finish. That's another fact. And I'm hung up on you, there's fact number three. Now maybe all of that irritates you, but that's the way it is. I'd like to start the interviews now."

He got to his feet as she did. "You're right. It all irritates me."

"There you go. I'd appreciate it if you'd send Will up now. And stay downstairs. I might need to speak with you again."

He came around the desk. Her eyes narrowed, flashed a cold warning as he approached her. They stayed level and cool when he gripped the lapels of her jacket and hauled her to her toes.

A dozen desires, all of them impossible, ran through his mind. "You push too many of my buttons," he muttered, and releasing her, walked away.

"Same goes." But she said it quietly, after he'd gone.

"So…" Frannie lit a cigarette, peered at Ally through the haze of smoke. "You're a cop. I might've figured it if Jonah hadn't been with you. He doesn't like cops any more than I do."

Frannie had put on an attitude, Ally noted, and nodded. "Now, there's breaking news.

Listen, let's make this as painless as possible for everyone. You've got the rundown on the burglary ring, how the club was used, Jan's part in it."

"I've got what you've decided to tell me now that you're wearing your badge."

"That's right. And that's all you need. How long have you known her?"

"About a year and a half, I guess. I ran into her in the laundry room of my apartment building. She was waiting tables in a bar, I worked in a bar." Frannie lifted her shoulders. "We hung out together now and again. I liked her well enough. When Jonah opened this place, I helped get her a job. Does that make me an accessory?"

"No, it makes you a jerk for copping an attitude with me. She ever mention a boyfriend?"

"She liked men, and men liked her."

"Frannie." Ally shifted, decided to play another angle. "Maybe you don't like cops, but there's one on the critical list right now, and he's a friend of mine. They're still not sure he'll make it. He's got two kids and a wife who loves him. Another woman's dead. Somebody loved her, too. You want to go a round with me on personal business, fine. Let's just get this done first."

Frannie made a little shrugging movement again. "She talked about this one guy sometimes. Never told me his name. Liked to be mysterious about it. But she said things like pretty soon she wouldn't be hauling trays and bagging tips."

She got up, crossed over to open the panel to the bar in a way that told Ally she was very at home in Jonah's space. She pulled out a soft drink, twisted off the cap. "I figured it was talk. She liked to talk big about men. Conquests, you know?"

"Did you ever see her with this guy?" Ally nudged the photo across the desk.

Sipping from the bottle, Frannie walked back, studied the photo. "Maybe. Yeah." Frannie scratched her jaw. "I saw them come into the building together a couple of times. Didn't seem like her type is what I thought. He's kinda short, a little pudgy. Ordinary. Jan, she went more for flash. Studs, with platinum cards was her usual type."

Catching herself, Frannie shook her head, dropped into a chair. "That sounds hard. I liked her. Look, she's young, maybe a little foolish. But she's not mean."

"You might want to keep in mind that she used you, Jonah, and this place. Now, did she ever mention anyplace they went together? Any plans?"

"No...well, she might've said something about a place on a lake. I didn't pay much attention when she started bragging. Most of it was just air."

Ally questioned her for another fifteen minutes, but didn't jiggle anything loose.

"Okay. If you think of anything, I'd appreciate a call." Rising, Ally offered Frannie a card.

"Sure." Frannie skimmed her eyes over it. "Detective Fletcher."

"Would you ask Beth to come up, please?"

"Why the hell don't you leave her alone? She doesn't know anything."

"But I have such a good time intimidating and threatening potential witnesses." She came around the desk, sat on the corner. "Okay, there's the bell. Go ahead with your personal round."

"I don't like the way you came in here, the

way you used us and spied on us. I know how it works. You did a background check on everybody, pried into all our lives and sat in judgment. I guess you're sorry it turned out to be Jan instead of the former hooker."

"You're wrong. I like you."

Off balance, Frannie sat again. "Bull."

"Why shouldn't I like you? You got yourself out of a spiral that only goes down. You've got a legitimate job, and you're good at it. The only problem I have with you is Jonah."

"What do you mean, Jonah?"

"You've got a relationship with him. I'm attracted to him. That's makes you a personal problem for me."

Baffled now, Frannie took out another cigarette. "I don't get you. You mean it about Jonah?" she said after a minute. "You've got a thing for him?"

"It looks like. But the problem's mine. Like I said, I like you. In fact, I admire the way you turned your life around. I never had to do that, never had to face those kinds of things, make those kind of choices. I'd like to think I'd do as well as you have if I had."

"Damn it." Frannie pushed to her feet, paced the room. "Damn it," she repeated. "Okay, first. I don't have a relationship with Jonah. Not like you mean. Never did. He never bought me when I was for sale, and he never touched me that way when I was free. Even when I offered."

Though a fine sense of relief ran through her, Ally kept her voice mild. "Is he blind or stupid?"

Frannie stopped pacing, took a long, hard look. "I don't want to like you. You're sure making it tough not to. I love him. A long time ago, I loved him…different than I do now. We grew up together, more or less. I mean we've known each other since we were kids. Me and Jonah and Will, we go back."

"I know. It shows."

"When I was working corners, Jonah'd come by sometimes, pay me for the night. Then he'd take me for coffee or something to eat. And that was it." Frannie's eyes softened. "He always was a sucker."

"Are we talking about the same man?"

"If he cares about you, that's it. He'll keep pulling you up no matter how many times you fall down again. Bite his hand, he'll just ignore you and haul you up. You can't fight that. You can't fight that kind of thing for long. I didn't make it easy for him."

With a sigh, she walked over to sit again, picked up the soft drink, finished it off. "A few years ago, I was scraping the bottom of the gutter. I'd been on the stroll since I was fifteen. By the time I hit twenty I was used up. So I figured what the hell, let's just get out of this whole mess. I started to slash my wrists. Seemed just dramatic enough."

She held out a hand, turned it over to expose the scar on the inside of her left wrist. "Only got to the one, and didn't do such a hot job on it."

"What stopped you?"

"First? The blood. Really put me off the idea," she said with a surprisingly cheerful laugh. "Anyway I'm standing there in this filthy bathroom, stoned, bleeding, and I got scared. Really scared. I called Jonah. I don't know what would've happened if I hadn't reached him, if he hadn't come. He got me to the hospital, then he got me into detox."

She sat back, tracing a finger over the scar as if it brought the memory back with more clarity. "Then he asked me something he'd asked me a hundred times before. He asked me if I wanted a life. This time I said yes. Then he helped me make one.

"Along the way, I thought I should pay him back, and I offered what I was used to offering men. It was the only time he ever really got pissed off." She smiled a little. "He thought more of me than I did of myself. Nobody else ever had. If I knew anything about Jan, or this business, I'd tell you. Because he'd want me to, and there's nothing I wouldn't do for him."

"From where I'm standing, you both got a good deal."

"I've never once had a man look at me the way I've seen him look at you."

"Then you've got your eyes shut." It was Ally's turn to smile. "Keep them open tonight when Will asks for his after-closing brandy."

"Will? Come on."

"Keep your eyes open," Ally said again. "Are we square here?"

"Yeah, sure. I guess." Confused, Frannie got to her feet again.

"Ask Beth to come up. Just give me five minutes to find my brass knuckles."

With a half laugh, Frannie went to the elevator. After pushing the button, she glanced back. "Will knows what I was."

"I guess he knows what you are, too."

She wrapped up the last interview by seven, circled her shoulders and wondered if there was a possibility of food any time in her near future.

The clock told her she was officially off duty, and since she had nothing to add to the current status of the case, her reports and follow-ups could wait till morning.

Still, she helped herself to the use of Jonah's phone, checking in, giving updates. She was sitting quietly at his desk when he came in.

"Dietz. The cop who was shot last night. They've upgraded his condition from critical to serious." Closing her eyes, she pressed her fingers against them. "It looks like he's going to make it."

"I'm glad to hear it."

"Yeah." She pulled the clip out of her hair, ran her fingers through it. "It sure fills this big hole in my gut. I appreciate the use of your office. I can tell you that the rest of your people aren't suspects, at this time."

"At this time."

"I can't give you more than that, Blackhawk. All evidence points to the fact that Jan and Jan alone worked the inside. It's the best I can do."

She tossed the clip on his desk. "Now, I've got something else to say."

"Which is?"

"I'm off duty. Can I have a drink?"

"I happen to have a club just downstairs."

"I was thinking of a private drink. From your private bar." She gestured toward the panel. "If you could spare a glass of wine. I noticed a nice sauvignon blanc in there."

He turned toward the panel, opened it, selected the bottle.

"Why don't you join me?"

"I'm still on duty. I don't drink during working hours."

"I noticed that. Don't drink, don't smoke,

don't hit on the customers. During working hours," she added.

He turned back, the glass of pale gold wine in his hand. And watched her take off her jacket.

"I hope you don't mind," she said, then shrugged out of her holster. "I find it awkward to seduce men when I'm wearing my weapon."

She laid it on his desk, then walked toward him.

Chapter 8

She might have taken off her gun, Jonah thought, but she wasn't unarmed. A woman with eyes as potent as whiskey and a voice like smoke would never be without a weapon.

Worse, she knew it. That longbow mouth was curved up, just a little, like a cat's when the canary cage was open. He didn't much care for his role as target.

"Your wine." He held out the glass, a deliberate move to keep an arm-span of distance between then. "And though I appreciate the thought, I don't have time for a seduction at the moment."

"Oh, it shouldn't take very long."

She imagined he'd devastated countless women with that careless, almost absent dismissal. For her, it was only a challenge she had every confidence of meeting.

She took the wine, and moved right in, grabbing a fistful of his shirt to hold him in place. "I really like the look of you, Blackhawk. Hot mouth, cool eyes." She took a sip of wine, watching him over the rim. "I want to see more."

His senses went blade sharp. The muscles of his belly tied themselves into a dozen hard and tangled knots. "You get right to it, don't you?"

"You said you were in a hurry." She rose on her toes to nip her teeth into his bottom lip, and sliced a jagged line of need straight through him. "So I'm picking up the pace."

"I don't like sexually aggressive women."

Her laugh was low, mocking. "You don't like cops, either."

"That's exactly right."

"Then this is going to be very unpleasant for

you. That's a shame." She leaned in, skimmed her tongue up the side of his neck. "I want you to touch me. I want you to put your hands on me."

He kept them at his sides, but in his mind they were already ripping at her shirt, already taking. "Like I said, it's a nice offer, but—"

"I can feel your heart pounding." She shook her hair back, and the scent of it slithered into his system. "I can feel the way you want me, the same way I want you."

"Some of us learn to shelve certain wants."

She saw the change in his eyes, the faintest deepening of green. Dead giveaway, she thought. "And some of us don't." She took another sip of wine, then moved forward, walking him backward. "I guess I'm going to have to get rough."

Mortified she'd put him in retreat, he stopped short, nearly groaning when her body bumped his. "You're going to embarrass yourself. Drink your wine, Detective Fletcher, and go home."

She imagined he thought his voice was clipped, dismissive. But it was thick and strained. And his heart was a fury under her fist.

"What is that answer you're always giving me? No. Yes, that's it." She drained her glass so the wine pumped in with the reckless power surging through her. "No," she said again and, tossing the glass aside, hooked a hand in the waistband of his trousers.

Aroused and furious, he retreated again. "Cut it out."

"Make me." She threw her head back, then leaped, arms wrapping around his neck, legs vised around his waist. "Come on and make me. You've got plenty of moves."

Her mouth swooped down to tease his, and she tasted a wild, wonderful mix of desire and temper. "Take me down," she whispered, raking her hands through his hair. "Finish it. Finish me."

His blood was raging. The taste of her, hot and female with the faint zip of wine, was on his tongue. "You're asking for trouble."

"So…" She rubbed her lips over his, as if imprinting her flavor on him. "Give it to me."

Control snapped. He could hear it echo in his head like the violent crack of hammer against stone. He gripped her hair, wrapping it around his hand, yanking it back so that she let out a little gasp as her head flew back.

"The line's crossed." His eyes weren't cool now. They simmered, as if a bolt of lightning had struck a pool. "You'll give me everything I want. What you don't give, I'll take. That's the deal."

Her breath was already quickened. "Done."

His gaze lowered to the long, vulnerable curve of her throat. Then he set his teeth on her.

Her body jerked against his as the shock of that threat of pain, that lance of pleasure stabbed into her. Then she was falling, clinging to him as she tumbled into the shadows, into the dark.

She lost her breath when she hit the bed, lost her grip when his body covered hers. Then, for a moment, when he tore her shirt open, she lost her mind.

Floundering for balance, she threw an arm up. Her knuckles thudded against the bedspread, then her fingers dug in. "Wait."

"No."

His mouth was on her breast, ravaging tender flesh with lips and teeth and tongue. She fought for air, fought to find the power that had been hers just moments before. Instead she found herself spinning past control, past reason.

His hands were on her, as she had demanded. And they were hard and fast, ruthlessly exploiting weakness, secrets she hadn't known she'd possessed.

Then his mouth came back to hers, hot and greedy. The low sound in her throat was equal parts terror and triumph. Leaping recklessly toward the heat, she met demand with demand.

She went wild beneath him. Writhing, bucking, reaching. He'd wanted nothing less. If he was to sin, he would sin fully, and reap all the pleasure before the punishment.

Her skin seemed to burn under his hands, his mouth. He craved. The long, clean lines of her. The taut and ready strength. The delicate give of curves.

He rolled with her over the wide pool of the bed, taking what and how he wanted.

She tugged at his shirt, sending buttons flying, then letting out a sound of feral delight when flesh met flesh. When he dragged her to her knees, she trembled. But there was nothing of fear left in her.

She could see his eyes, the predatory gleam of them, from the backwash of light from the office. She let out a ragged breath as she ran her hands up his chest, into his hair.

"More," she told him, and crushed her mouth to his.

And there was more.

Lightning quick flashes of unbearable ecstasy. Gusts of shuddering desperation. And a flood of needs that swamped them both.

He tugged the slacks down her hips, following the path of exposed flesh with his mouth until she was shuddering and mindlessly murmuring his name in that hoarse, erotic voice he couldn't get out of head.

His teeth scraped her inner thigh, sent the strong muscles quivering. When she arched, opened, he feasted on her.

She cried out as the orgasm ripped through her, fisted her hands in the bedclothes and let each glorious aftershock batter her until her system wept with the pleasure of it. Heat swarmed up her body, through her, and she embraced it, reveled in the breathless power of what they made together.

"Now. Jonah."

"No."

He couldn't get enough of her. Each time he thought desperation would overpower him, he found something new to tantalize him. The subtle flare of her hips, the narrow dip of her waist. He wanted to feel the bite of her nails on him again, hear that choked cry of release when he dragged her over the next edge.

Her breath was sobbing, his own so clogged in his lungs he thought they would burst from it. He moved up her again while her hands raced over him and her body bucked.

He could see her eyes, and nothing else. Just the dark glint of them, watching him as he rose over her. He held back for one quivering instant, then plunged.

Here was everything. The thought stabbed through him then shattered in his brain as she closed hot and tight around him.

She rose to him, fell with him, the slick slide of bodies mating. Sighed with him as pleasure shimmered. Her heart thundered against his, beat for beat. Their breath mixed, drawing him deeper so that his mouth was on hers, another link, as they moved together.

The tempo quickened so that the slide became a slap, and sighs broke into gasps and moans. Her hips pistoned as he pounded into her. As sensations staggered her, she raked her nails down his back, dug them into his hips. Urging him on even as she was swamped by the next crest.

He felt himself slip—a glorious feeling of surrender—and with his face buried in the tumbled mass of her hair, he fell.

It was over for him. He knew it the minute his system leveled and his mind began to work again. He'd never get over her. Never get past her. With one sweep, she'd destroyed a lifetime of careful avoidance.

Now he was stupidly, helplessly, irretrievably in love with her.

Nothing could be more impossible or more dangerous.

She could slice him to pieces. No one had ever been allowed to have that kind of control or power over him. He didn't mean to let that change now.

He needed some sort of defense, and determined to start building it, he rolled away from her.

She simply rolled with him, stretched that long, limber body of hers over his and said, "Mmmmm."

Another time he might have laughed, or at least felt that knee-jerk of pure male satisfaction. Instead he felt a light trip of panic.

"Well, you got what you wanted, Fletcher."

Instead of being insulted, which would have given him a little room to regroup, she just nuzzled his neck. "Damn right."

To please herself she hooked a leg around him, then shifted to straddle him and slick back her hair. "I like your body, Blackhawk. All tough and rangy and taut." She trailed a finger over his chest, admiring the contrast of her skin against his. "You've got some Native American blood, right?"

"Apache. Very diluted."

"It looks good on you."

He twirled a lock of her hair around his finger. "White bread," he said dryly. "But it looks good on you."

She leaned down until they were nose to nose.

"Now that we're all cozy and complimentary, how about doing me a favor?"

"And that would be?"

"Food. I'm starving."

"Want a menu?"

"No. Umm." She tilted her head, teased his mouth with hers. "Just something that's on it. Maybe you could send down for something." She trailed her lips down to his jaw, back up to his mouth. "And we could, you know, fuel up. Mind if I grab a shower?"

"No." He rolled her onto her back. "But you'll have to wait until I'm done with you."

"Oh?" She smiled. "Well, a deal's a deal."

And when he was done with her, she staggered more than walked into the bathroom. She closed the door, leaned back against it and let out a long puff of breath.

She'd never had to work harder to maintain a careless, sophisticated image. Then again, she'd never had anyone turn her inside out and leave her jittering like a mass of jelly before.

Not that she was complaining, Ally told

herself as she rubbed the heel of her hand over her heart. But her idea that sex was simply a pleasant occupation between two consenting adults who, hopefully, cared about each other had been forever shattered.

Pleasant didn't begin to describe making love with Jonah Blackhawk.

Waiting for her system to level again, she scanned the bathroom. He'd indulged himself here, she noted, with the deep, why-don't-you-join-me whirlpool tub in his customary jet-black. Though it looked tempting, she thought she'd settle for the separate shower enclosed by seeded glass.

The sink was a wide scoop in a sheer black counter. Nothing stood on it, no pieces of him left out for the casual eye to study. Just as there were no pieces, no odds and ends, memorabilia or personal photographs in his office or bedroom.

She was tempted to poke in the cabinet, rifle through a couple of the drawers—what kind of shaving cream did he use? What brand of tooth-paste?—but it seemed so pitifully obvious.

Instead she crossed the white tiles and studied

her own face in the mirror. Her eyes were soft, her mouth still swollen from that wonderful assault of his. There were a number of faint bruises shadowing her skin.

All in all, she decided she looked just the way she felt. Like a woman happily used.

But what did he see when he looked at her? she wondered. When he looked at her in that cool, distant way? He wanted her, she could have no doubts about that. But did he feel nothing else?

Did he think she hadn't noticed the way he'd drawn back from her both times, after passion had been spent? As if his need for…separation was as deep as his desire.

And why was she letting it hurt her? It was such a *female* reaction.

"Well, I am a female, damn it," she muttered and turned to switch on the shower.

If he thought he was going to get away with nudging her back whenever he pleased, he was very much mistaken. The man was not going to rock her to her toes then stroll away while she was still teetering.

She stuck her head under the spray, mumbling to herself.

She expected a lot more give-and-take in a relationship. And if he couldn't trouble himself to give her a little affection along with the heat, well then he could…

She trailed off, winced.

She sounded like Dennis, she thought. Or at least close enough.

At least she could stop that before she dug herself a hole too deep to crawl out of.

The only relationship she had with Jonah was a physical one, and she herself had insisted on it. Both of them knew the ground rules and were smart enough not to need them spelled out.

If she needed to mix emotion in with desire, that was fine. That was okay. But it was also her problem.

Satisfied she'd solved the matter in her own mind, she turned off the taps, turned for a towel.

And let out one wild yelp when she saw Jonah holding one out for her.

"Most people sing in the shower," he commented. "You're the first I've come across who talks to herself in the shower."

"I was not." She snatched the towel.

"Okay, it was more unintelligible mumbling."

"Fine. Most people knock before they come into an occupied bathroom."

"I did, but you couldn't hear me because you were talking to yourself. I thought you might want this." He held up his other hand, and the black silk robe that dangled from his fingers.

"Yeah. Thanks." She wrapped the towel around herself, anchored it with a hand between her breasts.

"Dinner'll be up in a minute." Idly he skimmed a fingertip down her arm, sliding water over flesh.

"Good. I need to get my weapon off your desk."

"I moved it." Frowning now, he traced the curve of her shoulder. "I put it in the bedroom. The door's closed. They'll just leave the tray on my desk."

"Works for me." When she felt the brush of his finger over her collarbone, she released her hold on the towel, let it fall to her feet. "Is this what you're looking for?"

"I shouldn't want you again already." Eyes on hers, he backed her against the wall. "I shouldn't need you again."

"Then walk away." She tugged down the zipper on the trousers he'd pulled on. "Who's stopping you?"

He closed a hand around her throat. Though the pulse under his fingers jumped, she merely lifted her chin and dared him.

"Tell me you want me," he demanded. "Say my name, and that you want me."

"Jonah." She took the first step onto a bridge she knew could burn away under her feet. "I've never wanted anyone the way I want you." Her breath hitched as she drew it in, but her eyes remained steady. "Give it back to me."

"Allison." He lowered his forehead to hers, in a gesture so weary and sweet, she reached out to comfort him. "I can't think for wanting you. Just you," he murmured, then took her mouth, took her body. Desperately.

"I gotta say," Ally commented as she ate like a starving wolf, "you've got a really good kitchen. A lot of clubs, the food's mediocre at best. But yours, um…'' She licked barbecue sauce from her thumb. "It's first-class."

She shook her head when he picked up the wine to top off her glass. "No, uh-uh. I'm driving."

"Stay." Another rule broken, he thought. He never asked a woman to stay.

"I would if I could." Smiling she tugged on the lapel of the borrowed robe. "But I don't have a change for tomorrow, and I'm back on eight-to-fours. As it is I'm going to have to borrow a shirt from you to get home. You did a number on mine."

He did no more than pick up his own glass, but she felt him retreat. "Ask me to come back tomorrow, and stay."

He looked back at her. "Come back tomorrow, and stay."

"Okay. Look at that! Look at that! That runner was safe."

"Out. By a half step," Jonah corrected, amused that she'd nearly come off the sofa when the play on the wide screen caught her eye.

"Bull. You watch the instant replay. They hit the bag at the same time. Tie goes to the runner. See? Manager's coming out. Give him hell. Anyway—"

Satisfied the requisite argument would proceed over a controversial call, she turned her attention back to Jonah. She smiled, rubbed her bare feet intimately against his hip. "Pretty good deal from my point of view. Good sex, good food and a ball game."

"To some…" He reached down to trace a finger up her instep. "Paradise."

"Since we're in paradise, can I ask you something really important?"

"All right."

"Are you going to eat all those fries?"

He grinned at her, shoved the plate in her direction, then leaned over to answer the phone. "Blackhawk. Yes." He held out the portable receiver. "For you, Detective."

"I left this number when I logged out," she told him, and took the phone. "Fletcher." She straightened on the sofa, and her eyes went flat. "Where? I'm on my way."

She was already on her feet when she tossed the receiver on the hook. "They found Jan."

"Where is she?"

"On her way to the morgue. I have to go."

"I'm going with you."

"There's no point in it."

"She worked for me," he said simply and walked into the bedroom.

Jonah had seen and done a great deal. In the first half of his life, he'd thought he'd seen and done everything. He'd seen death, but he'd never seen it stripped bare in cold, antiseptic surroundings.

He looked through the glass at the young woman and felt nothing but raw pity.

"I can verify ID," Ally said beside him. "But it's cleaner procedure if the visual comes from somebody else who knew her. Is that Janet Norton?"

"Yes."

She nodded to the technician behind the glass, and he lowered the blinds. "I don't know how long I'll be."

"I'll wait."

"There's coffee, down this corridor and to the left. It's crap, but it's usually hot and strong."

She reached for the door, hesitated. "Listen, if you change your mind and want to go, just go."

"I'll wait," he said again.

It didn't take her long. When she came out he was sitting in one of the molded plastic chairs at the end of the hallway. Her footsteps clicked on the linoleum, and the clicks echoed.

"Nothing much to do until the autopsy report's in."

"How did she die?" When Ally shook her head he got to his feet. "How? It can't be that big a dent in the rules to tell me."

"She was stabbed. Multiple wounds, by what appears to be a long bladed knife with a serrated edge. Her body was dumped on the side of the road off southbound 85, just a few miles outside of Denver. He threw her purse out with her. He wanted us to find her and ID her quickly."

"And that's it for you? Just identify her and put another piece in the puzzle?"

She didn't snap back. She recognized the chill in his eyes as temper on a short leash, and her own was straining.

"Let's get out of here." Ally headed out. She wanted to fill her lungs with fresh air. "From the number of wounds, it appears she was killed with considerable rage."

"Where's yours?" He shoved the door open. "Or don't you feel any?"

She strode out ahead of him. "Don't slap at me."

He grabbed her arm, whirled her around. She led with her fist and pulled it an inch from his jaw. "You want rage." She shoved away from him. "I'll give you some rage. From the looks of things she was getting sliced to pieces while I was rolling around on the sheets with you. Now ask how I feel?"

He caught her before she got to the car and wrenched the door open. "I'm sorry."

She tried to shrug him off, then push him away, but when she spun around snarling he just wrapped his arms around her.

"I'm sorry." He said it quietly, pressing his lips to her hair. "I was out of line. We both know it wouldn't have made any difference where we were or what we were doing. This would have happened."

"No, it wouldn't have made any difference. And still, two people are dead." She drew away. "I can't afford rage. Can you understand that?"

"Yes." He took the clip out of her hair, rubbed the back of her neck. "I'd like to go home with you. I'd like to be with you tonight."

"Good, because that's what I'd like, too."

She slid into the car, waiting for him to climb into the passenger seat. They both needed to set aside the rage, she knew, and the guilt. "I have to get up really early."

He smiled at her. "I don't."

"Okay." She pulled out of the lot. "That means you get to make up the bed and do the dishes. That's the deal."

"Does it also mean that you make the coffee?"

"It does."

"I'll take the deal."

When she reached her building, she pulled into the underground garage. "Tomorrow might be a long one," she told him. "Does it matter what time I get to your place?"

"No." He got out of the car, came around to her side, then held out his hand for her keys.

"So what, did you take like a charm school course or something?"

"Top of my class. I have a plaque." He pressed the button for the elevator. "Now some women are insecure and find the simple courtesy of a man opening doors for them or pulling out their chair, whatever, troubling. Naturally you're secure enough in your own power and femininity not to be troubled."

"Naturally," she agreed, and rolled her eyes as he gestured her into the elevator. Then he took her hand and made her smile.

"I like your style, Blackhawk. I haven't been able to pin it down, not exactly, but I like it." She angled her head to study him. "You used to play baseball, right?"

"That and your father kept me in high school."

"Basketball was my game. You ever shoot hoops?"

"Now and then."

"Want to shoot some with me, on Sunday?"

"I might." He walked out of the elevator with her. "What time?"

"Oh, let's say two. I'll pick you up. We can go—" She broke off, shifting in front of him fast and pulling her weapon. "Keep back. Don't touch anything."

He saw it now. The fresh scrape and pry marks on the door. She used two fingers on the knob, turned it, then booted the door open with her foot. She went in low, slapping the lights on, starting her sweep even as Jonah stepped in front of her.

"Get back. What are you crazy?"

"One of the things I learned in charm school was not to use a woman as a shield."

"This woman happens to be the one with the badge, and the gun."

"I noticed. Besides." He'd already scanned the debris of the room. "He's long gone."

She knew it, felt it, but there were rules and procedure. "Well pardon the hell out of me while I play cop and make sure. Don't touch anything," she said again, and stepping over a broken lamp, checked the rest of the apartment.

She was swearing in a low, steady voice as she headed for the phone.

"Your old friend Dennis?" Jonah asked.

"Maybe, but I don't think so. Lyle was heading south out of Denver." She jabbed her fingers into the keypad on the phone. "I think I just found out what he was doing here. This is Detective Fletcher. I've had a break-in."

Even before the crime scene unit arrived, Ally snapped on protective gloves and began to do inventory. Her stereo components, good ones, hadn't been stolen. But they had been smashed. Her laptop computer and the small TV that stood above the stereo had received the same treatment.

Every table lamp in the place—including the antique bookkeeper's light she'd bought for her desk—was broken. Her sofa had a long gash from end to end, and the guts of it spilled out in nasty puffs.

He'd poured the half gallon of paint she'd bought then had never gotten around to using, in the middle of her bed.

Over the bed, he'd slopped a message in the same paint.

Try To Sleep At Night

"He blames me for his sister's death. He knows I was the one. How does he know?"

"Jan," Jonah said from behind her. "She has to be the one who warned them something was wrong that night," he continued when Ally turned. "You got the Barneses back to their table, but they were still both gone for an unusual amount of time. They were nervous, upset. She picked up on it."

"Maybe." She nodded as she walked back out of the bedroom. "It was enough to make her start thinking. Worrying. She didn't notice when I left. She was busy, but Frannie did. She might have mentioned it to Jan in passing."

She picked her way through the living room, into the kitchen. "So she called it off, but just a little too late. Too late to save his sister. Doesn't look like he bothered much in here. Nothing worth smashing. I guess—" She broke off, walked slowly to the counter. "Oh God."

When she turned her eyes were wide and horrified. "My bread knife." She laid her fingertips on the knife block, with one empty slot. "Long blade with serrated edge. God, Jonah. He killed her with my own knife."

Chapter 9

She wasn't going to let it shake her. She couldn't. For a cop, she reminded herself, nerves were as costly as rage and just as dangerous. The break-in at her apartment was a direct, and personal, attack. Her only choice was to stand up to it, maintain her objectivity, and do the job she'd sworn to do.

When the crime scene unit had left, adding their wreckage to what Lyle had left behind him, she hadn't argued with Jonah. He'd told her to pack what she thought she needed.

She was moving in with him until it was over.

Neither of them talked about the giant step they were taking; they told themselves it was simply a logical and convenient arrangement.

Then they had slept, tangled together, for what was left of the night.

"We've doubled the guards on Fricks," Kiniki told her at the morning briefing. "Lyle can't get to him."

"He's too smart to try." Ally stood in her lieutenant's office, hands in pockets. The horror had dulled, and the thin edge of fear was over. "He can wait, and he will. He's not in any hurry to pay Fricks back for what he might see as his part in his sister's death."

Behind the glass wall of Kiniki's office, the phones in the bullpen rang, and detectives went about the business of the day. Ally put herself into the mind of a dead woman she'd known for a matter of days.

"Jan Norton was easy. It was all an adventure to her, romantic, exciting. She was with him, and thought she was safe with him. The canvass of my building turned up two neighbors who saw a couple fitting Lyle's and Jan's description enter the building at around eight o'clock. Holding hands," she added. "She helped him trash my place, then once they were on the road again, he killed her. She stopped having a purpose."

She'd had plenty of time to think it through, lying awake through the darkest hours of the night in Jonah's bed. "He doesn't do anything without a purpose. There's a lot of anger in him for what he sees as the privileged class. There's a pattern in his background, in his previous arrests. All of them involve crimes against wealth—the hacking, the burglaries. Even the assaults were against wealthy superiors at his job when he held a computer programming position."

She pulled her hands out of her pockets, ticked off her fingers. "Wealth, authority, authority, wealth. They're synonymous to him, and both need to be taken down a peg. He's smarter than they are. Why should they have the easy life?"

In her mind she flipped through the steadily growing file of data on Lyle Matthews. "He grew up on the bottom rung of lower middle class. Not quite poor, but never really comfortable. His father had a history of unemployment. Always moving from one job to another. His stepfather was arrogant and domineering. Lyle followed the same patterns. The supervisors and co-workers I've been able to contact all said the same basic thing. He's brilliant with tech stuff, but socially retarded. He's arrogant, belligerent and a loner. He came from a broken home, and both of his parents are dead. The only person he was ever close to was his sister."

Ally walked to the glass wall, looked out. "His sister played into his weaknesses, fed his monumental ego. One enabled the other. Now she's gone, and he's got no one but himself."

"Where would he go?"

"Not far," Ally calculated. "He's not finished yet. He has me to deal with, the Barneses, Blackhawk."

"I think your instincts are on target. We've put Mr. and Mrs. Barnes in a safe house. That leaves you, and Blackhawk."

She turned back. "I don't intend to take any unnecessary chances. But I have to keep visible, maintain a routine or he'll just go under and wait me out. He has my name, my address. He's probably got a reasonable description. He wants me to know it. To sweat it."

"We'll stake out your building."

"He may come back there. He doesn't want to just pick me off. It's not personal enough. And I don't think I'll be his first target."

"Blackhawk?"

"Yeah, in order of importance, Jonah's next. And as for Blackhawk, he's not cooperating."

And it still irked that he'd dismissed her idea of arranging protection.

"We can keep a couple of men on him, at a distance."

"You could keep them two miles away, and he'd spot them. Then he'd lose them on principle. Lieutenant, I'm…close to him. He trusts me. I can take care of it."

"You have an investigation to run, Detective, and your own butt to cover."

"I can do a considerable amount of all three at his club. And the fact is, I believe we might lure Lyle out, push him into making a move if he sees me with Blackhawk routinely."

"It's doubtful he knows you killed his sister. We've had a lid on that since the incident."

"But he knows I was part of the operation, the part inside the club. That Blackhawk and I worked together and started the steps that caused his sister's death."

"Agreed. I'm putting two men on Blackhawk, for the next seventy-two hours. Then we'll reevaluate."

"Yes, sir."

"On a different matter, you're aware that Dennis Overton's fingerprints were found on your hubcaps, your wheel wells. A search of his car turned up a recently purchased hunting knife. The lab work isn't back, but there were bits of tire rubber on the blade. He's been fired from the district attorney's office. They'd like to file formal charges."

"Sir—"

"Toughen your spine, Fletcher. If you don't file charges, he can walk. If you do, the D.A. will recommend psych evaluation. He needs it. Or do you want to wait until he shifts his obsession from you to somebody else?"

"No. No, I don't. I'll take care of it."

"Do it now. One lunatic out there after one of my detectives is enough."

The fact that he was right didn't make it any easier. Ally walked out to the squad room, plopped down at her desk and decided she deserved at least thirty seconds to brood.

She'd made mistakes with Dennis, right from the beginning. Hadn't paid enough attention, hadn't picked up on the cues. None of that was any excuse for his behavior, but it did weigh into her part in triggering it.

"What's the problem, Fletcher? The boss ream you?"

She glanced up at Hickman who made himself at home with his butt on the edge of her desk. "No. I'm about to ream somebody."

He bit into his midmorning Danish. "That usually puts me in a pretty chipper mood."

"That's because you're a heartless jerk."

"I love it when you flatter me."

"If I tell you you're a brainless moron, would you do me a favor?"

He took another bite, sprinkled crumbs on her desk. "My life for you, baby."

"I have to file on Dennis Overton. When the warrant comes through, would you pick him up? He knows you. It might be a little easier on him."

"Sure. Ally, he's not worth the regrets."

"I know it." She got to her feet, pulled her jacket from the back of her chair. Then she smiled, broke off a corner of his Danish and popped it into her mouth. "You're ugly, too."

"Girl of my dreams. Marry me."

Grateful Hickman knew how to lighten her mood, Ally headed out.

Two hours later she was walking into her father's office.

He met her at the door this time, ran his hands up and down her arms while he studied her face. Then he simply pulled her into his.

"Good to see you," he murmured.

She burrowed in, let herself absorb his strength, his stability. "You're always there, you and Mom. No matter what, you're right there. I just wanted to say that first."

"She's worried about you."

"I know. I'm sorry for it. Listen." She gave him an extra squeeze, then drew back. "I know you're up-to-date, but I wanted you to know I'm okay. And I'm handling it. Lyle can't wait long to make a move. He's got nobody now. Everything we've got on him indicates he needs somebody, a woman, to admire him, feed his ego, play his games with him. Alone, he'll break."

"I agree. And it's my assessment that it's a woman he'll want most to punish. You're elected."

"Agreed. He's already made his first big mistake by breaking into my place. He exposed himself. He left prints everywhere. His grief, his anger, pushed him to show me what he is and what he wants. Using my knife to kill Jan, that was his way of saying it could have been me."

"So far we have no argument. Why are you alone?"

"He won't move on me during the day. He works at night. I'm not going to take stupid chances, Dad. That's a promise. I wanted you to know I've filed charges against Dennis."

"Good. I don't want you hassled, and I don't want you distracted. I went by your apartment this morning."

"I've got some serious redecorating to do."

"You can't stay there. Come home for a few days. Until this is closed."

"I've, ah, already made arrangements." She tucked her hands into her pockets, rocked back on her heels. This part, she thought, would be tricky. "I'm staying at Blackhawk's."

"You can't bunk in a club," he began. Then it hit him, a sneaky jab to the solar plexus. "Oh." Boyd ran a hand through his hair, walked to his desk. Shook his head, walked to the coffeepot. "You, ah… Hell."

"I'm sleeping with Jonah."

His back still to her, Boyd lifted a hand, waved it from side to side. Acknowledging the signal, Ally closed her mouth and waited.

"You're a grown woman." He got that much out, then set the coffeepot back down. "Damn it."

"Is that a comment on my age, or my relationship with Blackhawk?"

"Both." He turned back. She was so lovely, he thought, this woman who'd come from him.

"Do you have anything against him?"

"You're my daughter. He's a man. There you

go. Don't grin at me when I'm having a paternal crisis."

Obediently she folded her lips. "Sorry."

"If you don't mind, I think I'll imagine you and Jonah are spending your time together discussing great works of literature and playing gin rummy."

"Whatever gets you through, Dad. I'd like to bring him to the Sunday barbecue."

"He won't come."

"Oh, yes." Ally smiled thinly. "He will."

She spent the rest of her shift doing follow-ups on the case and dealing with the threads of two others assigned to her. She closed one on sexual assault, opened another on armed robbery.

She parked her car in a secured lot and back-tracked the block and a half to Blackhawk's.

She spotted the stakeout car from the end of the block, and had no doubt Jonah had tagged it as well.

The first person she saw when she walked into the club was Hickman sitting hunched at the bar. She figured she could have spotted his black eye from a block away as well.

She went to him, tapped a finger under his chin and studied his face while he sulked. "Who popped you?"

"Your good friend and general jerk-face Dennis Overton."

"You're kidding. He resisted?"

"Ran like a jackrabbit." He glanced toward Frannie, tapped his glass for a refill. "Had to chase him down. Before I could cuff him, he caught me." He picked up his dwindling beer, sipped morosely. "Now I'm wearing this, and I've taken about all the razzing I'm going to."

"Sorry, Hickman." To prove it, she leaned over and touched her lips to the swollen bruise. When she leaned back, she noticed Jonah had turned the corner into the bar. He merely lifted a brow at seeing her with her arm around Hickman's shoulders, then signaled to Will.

"I never figured him for a rabbit." With a heavy sigh, Hickman scooped up a handful of bar nuts. "Then I take him down and got this." He shifted on the stool to show her the hole in the knee of his trousers. "And he's flopping around like a landed trout, and crying like a baby."

"Oh God."

"One ounce, one ounce of sympathy in his direction, Fletcher, and I'll pop you myself." Instead Hickman began popping the nuts into his mouth. "He swings back and his elbow catches me, right here, right on the cheekbone. I saw whole planets erupt. Stupid son of a bitch can do his crying in a cage tonight. What the hell'd you ever see in him?"

"Beats me. Frannie, put my pal's drinks on my tab, will you?"

"I'm switching to the imported stuff then."

She laughed, then glanced over her shoulder when Will came up behind her.

"Never used to have cops in here." But he said it with an easy smile, and winked at Frannie. "You want some ice on that eye, Officer?"

Hickman shook his head. "Nah." He used his good one to give Will the once-over. "You got a problem with cops?"

"Not in about five years. Say, is Sergeant Maloney still down at the sixty-third? He busted me twice. Was always straight about it."

Amused, Hickman turned around on the

stool. "Yeah, he's still there. Still working vice, too."

"You see him, you tell him, Will Sloan said hi. He was always square with me."

"I'll be sure to do that."

"Anyway, the man says I should have some dinner sent out to your friends in the Ford across the street. Figures they'll get hungry sitting out there all night twiddling their thumbs."

"I'm sure they'll appreciate that," Ally said dryly.

"Least we can do." Giving Hickman a friendly slap on the back, Will headed toward the kitchen.

"I've got a couple of things to do." Ally gave Hickman's black eye another look. "Put some ice on that," she advised, then made her way into the club area to track down Beth.

"Got a minute?"

Beth continued to key in codes on the register. "It's Friday night, we're booked solid. And we're a couple of waitresses short."

Ally acknowledged the sting of the cool tone, but didn't back down. "I can wait until your break."

"I don't know when I'll be able to take one. We're busy."

"I'll wait. I won't take up much of your time."

"Suit yourself." Without a glance at her, Beth strode away.

"She's feeling pretty raw," Will commented.

Ally turned around. "Are you everywhere?"

"Mostly." He lifted his shoulders. "That's my job. She trained Jan like, you know, she trained you. I guess we're all pretty shaken up about what happened."

"And blaming me?"

"I don't. You were doing your job. That's how it works. Beth, she'll come around. She thinks too much of the man not to. You want me to get you a table? Band's going to start in about an hour, and it's a hot one so there won't be a square inch of free space if you wait."

"No, I don't need a table."

"Give a yell if you change your mind."

"Will." She touched his arm before he could walk away. "Thanks."

He gave her a wide, easy smile. "No problem. I got nothing but respect for cops. In the last five years."

Beth made her wait an hour, and Ally was having her eardrums rattled by the band's second number, when the head waitress quickly strode up to her.

"I've got ten minutes. You can have five of them. That'll have to be enough."

"Fine." She had to lift her voice to a shout. "Can we go back in the employee lounge, or would you rather yell at each other right here?"

Saying nothing, Beth spun around and marched out of the club area. She unlocked the door to the lounge, walked to the sofa and, sitting, took off her shoes.

"More questions, Detective Fletcher?"

Ally closed the door and shut off the worst of the racket behind it. "I'll keep it brief and to the point. You're aware of what happened to Jan?"

"Yes. I'm very aware of it."

"Her next of kin have been notified," Ally said in the same flat tone. "Her parents will be in Denver tomorrow, and would like her things. I'd like to box up whatever she might have in her locker, and have it available for them. It would be easier on them that way."

Beth's lips trembled, and she looked away. "I don't have the combination to her lock."

"I do. She had it written down in her address book."

"Then do what you have to do. You don't need me."

"I need a witness. I'd appreciate it if you'd verify that I list any and all items in her work locker, that I put nothing in from the outside, or misappropriate any of her property."

"That's all it is to you? All what happened to her is to you? Another bit of business?"

"The sooner I cover every bit of business, the sooner we find the man who did this to her."

"She was nothing to you. None of us were. You lied to us."

"Yes, I lied. And since under the same circumstances I'd lie again, I can't apologize for it."

Ally walked to the locker, spun the combination lock. "To your knowledge did anyone have the combination to this except Janet Norton?"

"No."

Ally removed the lock, opened the door. As she scanned the contents, she took a large evidence bag from her purse.

"It smells like her." Beth's voice trembled, then broke. "You can smell her perfume. Whatever she did, she didn't deserve to be killed, to be thrown out on the side of the road like trash."

"No, she didn't. I want the man who did it to her to pay as much as you do. More."

"Why?"

"Because there has to be justice, or there's nothing. Because her parents loved her, and their hearts are broken. Because I can smell her perfume. Cosmetic bag," Ally snapped out, grabbing the hot-pink case, yanking the zipper. "Two lipsticks, powder compact, three eyeliner pencils—"

She broke off when Beth touched her arm. "Let me help you. I'll write it down."

She took a tissue out of her pocket, wiped her eyes, then stuffed it away again to take out her pad. "I liked you, you see. I liked who I thought you were. It was a kind of an insult to find out you were someone else."

"Now you know. Maybe we can start from here."

"Maybe." Beth pulled out her pencil and began to write.

* * *

Ally ordered a light meal at the bar and kept her eye on Jonah. His Friday night crowd was thick and they were rowdy. The longer she sat, watching, listening, the more she began to see the myriad problems of keeping him safe.

She saw just as many problems convincing him he needed to make adjustments in his life-style until Matthew Lyle was in custody.

Because she considered herself on duty, she stuck with coffee. And when the caffeine started to jiggle her system, switched to bottled water.

When the inactivity threatened to drive her mad, she informed Frannie she was going to help out with the bar tables and grabbed a tray.

"I believe I fired you," Jonah said as she hauled a tray of empties to the bar.

"No, you didn't. I quit. House draft and a bump, Pete, campari and soda, Merlot with ice on the side and the complimentary ginger ale for the designated driver."

"You got it, Blondie."

"Go upstairs, get off your feet. You're tired."

Ally merely narrowed her eyes at Jonah's

orders. "Pete, this guy's making insulting remarks about my looks. And he just put his hand on my butt."

"I'll break his face for you, honey, just as soon as I have a free hand."

"My new boyfriend here has biceps like oil tankers," Ally warned Jonah, and executed a stylish hair flip. "So you better watch your step, pretty boy."

He grabbed her chin, lifted her to her toes by it, then kissed her until her eyes threatened to roll back in her head. "I'm not paying you," he said mildly and strolled away.

"I'd work for that kind of tip," the woman on the stool beside her commented. "Anytime, anywhere."

"Yeah." Ally let out a long breath. "Who wouldn't?"

She worked through last call, then grabbed a table in the club and put her feet up while the band broke down and the staff prepared for closing.

And sitting, fell asleep.

Jonah sat across from her while the club went quiet.

"Anything I can do for you before I head out?"

He glanced up at Will. "No. Thanks."

"Guess she's worn-out."

"She'll bounce back."

"Well…" Will jiggled the change in his pockets. "I'm just going to have my nightcap, then head home. I'll see Frannie off and lock up. See you tomorrow."

The man was sunk, was all Will could think as he walked back to the bar. Who could've figured it? The man was sunk, and over a cop.

"A cop." Will slid onto a stool. On cue, Frannie set down his nightly brandy. "The man's hooked on the cop."

"You just clued into that?"

"I guess." He tugged on his beard. "You think it'll work out?"

"I'm no judge of romantic relationships. They look good together, though, and they won't be able to run over each other since both of them have heads like bricks."

"She conked out in there." Will jerked his head toward the club, then sipped his brandy. "He's just sitting, watching her sleep. I think you can mostly tell what's going on in a man by the way he watches a woman."

And because he caught himself watching Frannie as she mopped up the bar, he flushed and stared down at his drink as if the brandy suddenly contained the solution to a very complex problem.

But she caught it, this time she caught it because she was looking for it. She continued to wipe the bar dry as she inventoried her reaction. A nice little tug, she realized, and just a little heat to go with it.

She hadn't felt—or hadn't let herself—feel either for a man in a very, very long time.

"I guess you're heading home," she said casually.

"I guess. You?"

"I was thinking about ordering a pizza and watching this horror movie marathon on cable."

He smiled over at her. "You always had a thing for monster movies."

"Yeah. Nothing like giant tarantulas or blood-sucking vampires to chase away your troubles. Still… It's not a lot of fun by myself. You up for it?"

"Up for—" Brandy sloshed over the rim of his snifter and onto her clean bar. "Sorry. Damn. I'm clumsy."

"No, you're not." She slid the cloth over the spilled brandy, then looked him dead in the eye. "Do you want to split a pizza with me, Will, and watch old black-and-white monster movies, and neck on my sofa?"

"I— You—" He'd have gotten to his feet if he could have felt them. "Are you talking to me?"

She smiled, spread her cloth over the rim of the bar sink. "I'll get my jacket."

"I'll get it." He pushed to his feet, relieved when they held him upright. "Frannie?"

"Yes, Will?"

"I think you're beautiful. I just wanted to say that right out in case I'm too nervous later and forget."

"If you forget later, I'll remind you."

"Yeah. Okay. Good. I'll get your jacket," he said, and leaving her grinning, dashed off.

Jonah waited until the club was empty, until he heard Will and Frannie call out their good-nights. He rose, leaving Ally sleeping as he checked the locks and alarms himself. His heels clicked on the silver floor as he crossed it to go backstage. He chose the light pattern and music loop that suited his mood, and set them.

Satisfied, he went back to Ally and bending down, kissed her awake.

She floated to the surface on the taste of him. Warm, a little rough, and very ready. When she opened her eyes, it was as though a thousand stars were twinkling against the night.

"Jonah."

"Dance with me." His mouth continued to nibble on hers as he lifted her to her feet.

She already was. Before the clouds cleared from her brain, she was moving with him, body molded to body as music rippled around them.

"The Platters." She stroked her cheek against his. "That's so weird."

"You don't like it? I can put on something else."

"No, I love it." She angled her head to give his lips freer access to her neck. "This number, it's my parents' song. *Only You.* You know my mother was a night shift DJ at KHIP before she was station manager there. This is the song she played over the radio for my father the night she agreed to marry him. It's a nice story."

"I've heard pieces of it."

"You should see the way they look at each other when they dance to this. It's beautiful."

She dipped her fingers into his hair as they glided over the stars in the floor. "Very smooth," she whispered. "You're very smooth, Blackhawk. I should've figured it." She turned her head on his shoulder, watched the lights gleam. "Is everyone gone?"

"Yes." There's only you, he thought, brushing his lips over her hair. Only you.

Chapter 10

For the first time in weeks Ally woke without the need to jump out of bed and rush into the day.

Glorious Sunday.

Since Saturday night at Blackhawk's had been more crowded than the night before, she'd spent most of the time on her feet, and all of it mentally on duty.

Jonah might have shrugged off the guards outside the club, but she didn't think he'd take having her standing as his shield quite so casually.

Some things were best left undisclosed and undiscussed.

Besides, they were doing each other a favor. She couldn't stay in her apartment until it was cleaned out and refurnished. He was giving her a comfortable place to stay, and she was giving him a bodyguard. To her, it was a fair and rational deal.

And the deal had a distinctively superior side benefit. Intent on indulging in it, she ran her hand over his chest and began to nibble on the body she was more than happy to shield and protect.

He shot awake, fully aroused, with her mouth hot and greedy on his.

"Let me. Let me." Exhilarated, she chanted it, already straddling him, already riding. She hadn't known her blood could leap so fast, that her own needs could bolt from lazy to desperate in one hammer beat of the heart.

She took him in, surrounded him, her own body shuddering and bowing back as the sharp claws of pleasure raked her.

He kept the bedroom dark. It was all shadows and movement as he reared up to wrap his arms around her. Possession. It drove them both. He found her mouth, her throat, her breast, fed the hunger she'd unleashed in him before he could think, before he could do anything but feel.

Her release came like a whiplash, snapping and slicing the system. And when she melted against him, he laid her back. Began to love her.

A kiss, soft as the shadows. A touch, tender as the night. When she reached for him, he took her hands, cupping them together and bringing them to his lips in a gesture that had something rich, something sumptuous sliding through her to tangle with needs still raw.

"Now let me."

This was different. This was patient and sweet and slow. A fire banked and left to simmer with light.

She yielded herself, a surrender as powerful as seduction. He was murmuring to her, quiet words that stirred the soul even as he stirred her blood. As her breathing thickened she floated on the thin and delicate layers of silky sensations.

The brush of his fingertips, of his hair, the warmth of his lips, the glide of his tongue urged her higher, gradually higher. As the rise of desire became a deep and liquid yearning that spread to an aching need, she moaned his name.

He slid her over the first satin edge.

He needed to touch her this way, to take her this way. He needed, at least in the shadows, to have the right to. Here, she could belong to him.

Her arms came around him as he sank into a kiss, took it deep, fathoms deeper, until he was lost in it. And lost, he slipped inside her, held there linked, and desperately, helplessly in love.

When at last they lay quiet, she turned her face into his throat, wanting the taste of him to linger just a little longer. "No, don't move," she whispered. "Not yet."

Her body was gold, pulsing gold. She would have sworn even the dark had gilt edges.

"It's still night." She stroked her hands down his back, up again. "As long as we're like this, it's still night."

"It can be night for as long as you want."

Her lips curved against him. "Just a little longer." She sighed again, content to hold and be held. "I was going to get up and use your equipment, but then…well, there you were, and it just seemed like a much better idea to use you."

"Good thinking." He closed his eyes and kept her close.

She let the morning slide away, enjoyed a fast, hard workout with him in his gym while they argued over sports' highlights that flashed by on the portable TV.

They shared a breakfast of bagels and coffee, along with the Sunday paper, while spread out lazily in bed. Natural, normal, almost domestic habits, Ally thought as they dressed for the day.

Not that a man like Blackhawk could or should be domesticated. But a slow, uncomplicated Sunday morning was a nice change of pace.

She sat on the side of the bed and laced up her ancient high-tops. Jonah tugged on a T-shirt, studied the endless line of her legs.

"Is your plan to wear those little shorts to distract me from whipping your excellent ass on the court?"

She lifted both eyebrows. "Please. With my innate skill I don't need such pitiful ploys."

"Good, because once I start a game, nothing distracts me until my opponent is crushed."

She stood, rolled strong shoulders shown to advantage in the sleeveless jersey. "We'll see who's crushed, Blackhawk, when the buzzer sounds. Now are you going to stand around here bragging, or are you ready to rock and roll?"

"More than ready, Detective Honey."

She waited until they were in his car. She thought the timing best. Besides, the longer she waited to bring it up, the shorter amount of time he'd have to argue with her.

Casually, she stretched out her legs and prepared to enjoy the ride. And smirked, just a little, when she saw his gaze shift, and slide down the length of her legs.

"So, are you ever going to let me drive this machine?"

Jonah switched on the engine. "No."

"I can handle it."

"Then buy your own Jag. Where's the court where you want to go down in inglorious defeat?"

"You mean where's the court where I plan to beat you into a whimpering pulp of humiliation? I'll give you directions. Of course, if I were driving, I could just take us there."

He merely flicked her a pitying glance, then slipped on his sunglasses. "Where's the court, Fletcher?"

"Out near Cherry Lake."

"Why the hell do you want to shoot hoops way out there? There are a half-dozen gyms around here."

"It's too nice a day to play indoors. Of course if you're afraid of a little fresh air…"

He reversed, and drove out of the parking lot.

"What do you do besides use that gorgeous equipment in your apartment over the club when you have a free day?" she asked him.

"Catch a game, check out a gallery." He sent her a slow smile. "Pick up women."

She tipped down her own sunglasses, peered at him over the tops. "What kind of game?"

"Depends on the season. If it's got a ball or a puck, I'll probably watch it."

"Me, too. I've got no resistance. What kind of gallery?"

"Whatever appeals at the time."

"You've got some great art. In the club and in your apartment."

"I like it."

"So… What kind of women?"

"The easy kind."

She laughed and tucked her glasses back in place. "You calling me easy, ace?"

"No, you're work. I like a change of pace now and again."

"Lucky me. You've got a lot of books," she commented. She studied his profile, the sexy, angular lines of it, the way the dark glasses concealed the fascinating contrast of those eyes of pure, light green. "It's hard to picture you curling up with a good book."

"Stretching out," he said, correcting her. "Women curl up with books, guys stretch out."

"Oh, I see. That's entirely different. This is your exit coming up. You'll take the two-two-five. And watch your speed. The traffic cops just love to nail pretty boys like you in their hot cars."

"I have pull in the police department."

"You think I'm going to fix a ticket for you when you won't even let me drive this thing?"

"It so happens I know the police commissioner."

As soon as he said it, it clicked.

"You said out in Cherry Lake?"

"That's right."

He got off the first exit and pulled into a convenience store parking lot.

"Problem?"

"Your family lives in Cherry Lake."

"That's right. And they have a basketball court—well half court. It was all we could push my parents into, even though my brothers and I campaigned pretty hard. They also have a barbecue pit, which my father puts to very good use. We try to get together a couple Sundays a month."

"Why didn't you tell me we were going to your parents'?"

She recognized the tone: anger, ruthlessly tethered. "What difference does it make?"

"I'm not intruding on your family." He shoved the car in reverse again. "I'll drop you off. You can get a ride back when you're done."

"Hold on." She reached over, switched off the ignition. If he was angry, fine, they'd fight.

But she'd be damned if he'd freeze her out. "What do you mean intruding? We're going to shoot some baskets, eat some steak. You don't need an engraved invitation."

"I'm not spending Sunday afternoon with your family."

"With a cop's family."

He pulled his sunglasses off, tossed them aside. "That has nothing to do with it."

"Then what does? I'm good enough to sleep with, but I'm not good enough for this?"

"That's ridiculous." He shoved out of the car, stalked to the end of the lot and stared out on a narrow grassy area.

"Then tell me something that isn't ridiculous." She marched up to him, jabbed his shoulder. "Why are you so angry that I want you to spend a few hours with my family?"

"You conned me into this, Allison. That's first."

"Why should I have to con you into it? Why is it, Jonah, that you've known my father for more than half your life but you've never accepted a single invitation to our home?"

"Because it's his home, and I have no place

there. Because I owe him. I'm sleeping with his daughter, for God's sake."

"I'm aware of that. So is he. What? Do you think he's going to dig out his police issue and shoot you between the eyes when you walk in the door?"

"This isn't a joke. It's so easy for you, isn't it?"

Here's the heat, she thought, pumping.

"Everything was always just right in your world. Solid, balanced and steady. You have no idea what mine was before he came into it, and what it would be now if he hadn't. This is not the way I intend to pay him back."

"No, you pay him back by insulting him. By refusing to acknowledge your relationship with me, as if it was something to be ashamed of. You think I don't know what your life was like? You think my world was so rarefied, Blackhawk. I'm the daughter of a cop. There's nothing you've seen I haven't, through his eyes. And now my own."

She drilled a finger in his chest. "Don't you talk up to me, and don't you talk down. Wherever, however each of us started, we're on level ground now. And you'd better remember it."

He grabbed her hand. "Stop poking at me."

"I'd like to flatten you."

"Same goes."

He walked away, waiting until he was sure he had some level of control again. Her mention of shame had gotten through. He could be angry with himself for falling in love with her. But he wouldn't be ashamed of it.

"I'll make you a deal. You get rid of the tail." He gestured to the shadow car that had pulled in a minute behind them. "And we'll take a couple of hours at your parents'."

"Give me a second."

She walked to the dark sedan, leaned in and had a short conversation with the driver. She had her hands in her pockets as she strode back over to Jonah.

"I cut them loose for the rest of the afternoon. It's the best I can do." She circled her shoulders. Apologies always tensed her up. "Look, I'm sorry I played it this way. I should have done it straight and we could have argued about it back at your place."

"You didn't play it straight because you knew I wouldn't be here to argue with."

"Okay, you're right." She threw up her hands in defeat. "Sorry again. My family's important to me. I'm involved with you. It just follows that I want you to feel comfortable with them."

"Comfort might be asking a little too much. But I'm not ashamed of my relationship with you. I don't want you to think I am."

"Fair enough. Jonah, it would mean a lot to me if you'd give it a try this afternoon."

"It's easier to argue with you when you're being obnoxious."

"Now see, that's what my brother Bryant always says. You'll get along fine." Hoping to soften things, she hooked her arm with his. "There's one thing, though," she began as they walked back to the car.

"What thing?"

"This deal at the house today? It's a little…more than I might have indicated. Sort of a kind of reunion. It's just that there'll be more people, that's all," she said quickly. "Aunts and uncles and cousins from back east, and my father's old partner and her family. It's really better for you this way," she insisted when he balled a fist and tapped it against her chin. "It's more a horde than a group, so nobody'll even notice you. Hey, why don't you let me drive the rest of the way?"

"Why don't I knock you unconscious and you can ride in the trunk the rest of the way?"

"Never mind. It was just a thought." She strolled around the car, reached for the door handle. But he beat her to it. It made her laugh, and turn and take his face in her hands.

"You're a real case, Blackhawk." She gave him a noisy kiss, then climbed in. When he joined her, she leaned over, rubbed her knuckles over his cheek. "They're just people. Really nice people."

"I don't doubt it."

"Jonah. An hour. If you're uncomfortable being there after an hour, just tell me. I'll make an excuse and we'll go. No questions. Deal?"

"If I'm uncomfortable in an hour, I'll go. You stay with your family. That's the way it should be, so that's the deal."

"All right." She settled back, secured her belt. "Why don't I give you a quick rundown so you know the players? There's Aunt Natalie and her husband—Ryan Piasecki. She runs some of the interests of Fletcher Industries, but her real baby is Lady's Choice."

"Underwear?"

"Lingerie. Don't be a peasant."

"Terrific catalogues."

"Which you peruse for fashion's sake."

"Hell no. There are half-naked women in there."

She laughed, relieved they'd passed the crisis point. "Moving right along. Uncle Ry's an arson inspector in Urbana. They have three kids, fourteen, twelve and eight, if my math's right. Then there's my mother's sister, Aunt Deborah—Urbana's district attorney—her husband, Gage Guthrie."

"The Guthrie who has more money than the national treasury?"

"So rumor has it. Four kids for them. Sixteen, fourteen and twelve, ten. Like steps." She made upward motions with her hand. "Then there's Captain Althea Grayson, Dad's former partner, and her husband Colt Nightshade. Private Investigator. More of a troubleshooter really. Sort of a loose cannon. You'll like him. They have two kids, one of each, fifteen and twelve. No, thirteen now."

"So basically, I'm spending the afternoon with a teenage baseball team."

"They're fun," she promised him. "You don't like kids?"

"I have no idea. My exposure to their species has been limited."

"This exit," she told him. "Well, it won't be limited after today. I think you might have met my brothers somewhere along the line. Bryant's in Fletcher Industries. I guess he's a kind of troubleshooter, too. Does a lot of traveling and nailing butts to the wall. He loves it. And Keenan's a firefighter. We visited my aunt Natalie right after she hooked up with Uncle Ry, and Keen, he fell for the big red truck. That was it for him. Left at the next light. That wraps it up."

"I have a headache."

"No, you don't. Right at the corner, left two blocks down."

He'd already gotten a solid impression of the neighborhood. Stable, rich and exclusive with its big, beautiful houses on big, beautiful grounds. It gave him an itch between the shoulder blades he'd never be able to explain.

He was comfortable in the city, where the streets reminded him he'd overcome something, and the faces that crowded him were anonymous. But here, with the majestic trees, the sloped lawns, green and lush with approaching summer, the explosion of flowers and rambling old homes, he wasn't just a stranger.

He was an intruder.

"That one there, on the left, the cedar and river rock, with the zigzagging decks. I guess everyone's here already. Looks like a parking lot."

The double driveway was packed. The house itself was a huge and unique study of rooflines, jutting decks, wide expanses of glass, all accented by trees and flowering bushes with a meandering slate path ribboning up the gentle hill.

"I've reassessed the deal," Jonah told her. "I'm adding exotic sexual favors. I think this deserves them."

"Fine. I'll take 'em."

She reached for the door, but his arm shot

out, pinned her back against the seat. She only laughed and rolled her eyes. "Okay, okay, we'll discuss exotic sexual favors later. Unless you're demanding a down payment on them here and now."

"Yeah, that'll put a cap on it." He jerked open his door, but before he could walk around the car, there was a war whoop, and a pretty young girl with a pixie cap of dark hair raced down the hill.

She grabbed Ally in a bear hug the minute she was out of the car. "There you are! Everyone's here. Sam already pushed Mick into the pool and Bing chased your neighbor's cat up a tree. Keenan got him down and my mom's inside putting something on the scratches. Hi."

She beamed a hundred-watt smile at Jonah. "I'm Addy Guthrie. You must be Jonah. Aunt Cilla said you were coming with Ally. You own a nightclub? What kind of music do you have?"

"She does shut up twice a year, for five minutes. We time it." Ally wrapped an arm around her cousin's neck and squeezed. "Sam is in the Piasecki branch, Mick is Addy's brother. And Bing is our family dog who has no manners whatsoever, so he fits in very well. Don't worry about remembering any of that, or you really will have a headache."

She reached out to take his hand, but Addy beat her to it. "Can I come to your club? We're not going home until Wednesday. Thursday if nagging works. I mean what's one more day? Gosh, you're really tall, aren't you? He looks great, too," she added peering around him to her cousin. "Nice job, Allison."

"Shut up, Addy."

"Somebody's always saying that to me."

Charmed despite himself, Jonah smiled at her. "Do you listen?"

"Absolutely not."

The noise level rose—screams, shouts. A couple of gangly teenagers of indeterminate sex raced by armed with enormous water guns. He saw a woman with a sunny sweep of hair in deep conversation with a striking redhead. A group of men—some stripped to the waist—battled it out brutally on a blacktopped basketball court. Another group of young people, dripping wet, raided a table loaded with food.

"Pool's around the other side of the house," Ally explained. "It's glassed in so we can use it all year."

One of the men on court pivoted, drove through the line of defense and dunked the ball. Then he caught sight of Ally, and deserted the field.

She met him halfway, shouting with laughter when he plucked her off her feet. "Put me down, moron. You're sweaty."

"So would you be if you were leading your team to a second consecutive victory." But he dropped her on her feet, wiped his hand on his jeans, then held it out to Jonah. "I'm Bryant, Ally's far superior brother. Glad you could make it. Want a beer?"

"Yes, actually."

Bryant eyed Jonah, measuring size and build. "You play any round ball?"

"Occasionally."

"Great, we're going to need fresh meat. Shirts and skins. Ally, get the man a beer while I finish trouncing these pansies."

"Come on inside." In a show of sympathy, Ally rubbed a hand up and down Jonah's arm.

"Get your bearings. It's too confusing to try to meet everyone at once."

She drew him up onto a deck, where yet another table was spread with food and an enormous metal trough was filled with ice and cold drinks. She plucked out two beers and went in through the atrium doors.

The kitchen was spacious, broken up into family areas with counters and a banquette. In one corner a dark-haired man was trying to tug away from a dark-haired woman. "I'll live, Aunt Deb. Mom, get her off me."

"Don't be a baby." With her head stuck in the refrigerator, Cilla swore. "We're going to run out of ice. I knew it. Didn't I tell him we'd run out of ice?"

"Hold still, Keenan." Deborah covered the scratches with a gauze pad, taped it neatly. "There, now you can have a lollipop."

"I'm surrounded by smart alecks. Hey, speaking of which, here's Ally."

"Aunt Deb." Ally hurried over to hug her aunt, then reached over and grazed her knuckles over Keenan's cheek. "Hi, hero. This is Jonah Blackhawk. Jonah, my aunt, Deborah, my brother, Keenan. You've met my mother."

"Yes. Nice to see you again, Mrs. Fletcher."

A small army chose that moment to pour in through the door, full of shouted complaints and chased by an unbelievably large and ugly dog.

Ally was immediately absorbed into them. And before he could defend himself, so was Jonah.

Jonah intended to leave at the end of the hour. A deal was a deal. His plan was to make some polite conversation, keep as far out of the way as humanly possible, then fade back, into his car, and back into the city where he knew the rules.

And somehow, he was stripped out of his shirt and going elbow to gut in a vicious game of basketball with Ally's uncles, cousins, brothers. In the heat of competition, he lost track of intentions.

But he damn well knew it was Ally herself who stomped on his instep and cost him game point.

She was fast and sneaky, he conceded that as he ripped the ball away from an opponent and gave her one deadly glare. But she hadn't grown up on the streets where a single basket could mean a buck for a burger against a painfully empty stomach.

That made him faster. And sneakier.

"I like him." Natalie ignored her son's blood-curdling scream of revenge and tucked an arm through Althea's.

"He was a hard-ass, but Boyd always liked him. Ouch, he plays dirty."

"What other way is there? Whoa, Ryan's going to be limping tomorrow. Serves him right," Natalie said with a laugh. "Taking on a guy half his age. Nice butt."

"Ry's? I've always thought so."

"Keep your eye off my husband, Captain. I was referring to our Ally's young man."

"Does Ryan know you ogle young men?"

"Naturally. We have a system."

"Well, I am forced to agree. Ally's young man has a very nice butt. Oh, ouch, that had to hurt."

"I think I could take him," Natalie murmured, then laughed at Althea's arch look. "In basket-ball. Get your mind out of the gutter." She swung an arm over her old friend's shoulder. "Let's go get some wine and pump Cilla for info on this new and very interesting situation."

"You read my mind."

"I know nothing, I say nothing," Cilla claimed as she poured another bag of ice into the trough. "Go away."

"It's the first guy she's brought to one of the family deals," Natalie pointed out.

Cilla merely straightened and mimed zipping her own lips.

"Give it up," Deborah advised. "I've been interrogating her for a half hour, and I got zero."

"You lawyers are too soft." Althea moved forward, grabbing Cilla by the collar. "Now a good cop knows how to get to the truth. Spill it, O'Roarke."

"Do your worst, copper, I ain't no stool pigeon. Besides, I don't know anything yet. But I will," she murmured as she saw Ally dragging Jonah toward the deck. "Clear out, give me five minutes."

"It's nothing," Jonah insisted.

"It's blood. Rules of the house. If it bleeds, it gets mopped up."

"Ah, another victim." Cilla rubbed her hands together as her friends and relations conveniently scattered. "Bring him on."

"His face ran into something."

"Your fist," Jonah said with some bitterness. "Guarding the goal doesn't include left jabs."

"Around here it does."

"Let's see." Wisely Cilla kept her expression sober as she studied Jonah's bleeding lip. "Not so bad. Ally go help your father."

"But I—"

"Go help your father," Cilla repeated, and snagging Jonah's hand dragged him up to the deck and into the kitchen. "Now let's see, where did I put my instruments of torture?"

"Mrs. Fletcher."

"Cilla. Sit down, and button it up. Whining is severely punished around here." She gathered up a damp cloth, ice and antiseptic. "Punched you, did she?"

"Yes, she did."

"Takes after her father. Sit," she ordered again and jabbed a finger into his bare stomach until he obeyed. "I appreciate your restraint in not hitting her back."

"I don't hit women." He winced when she dabbed at the cut.

"Good to know. She's a handful. Are you up to that?"

"I beg your pardon?"

"Is it just sex, or are you up for the whole package?"

He wasn't sure which shocked him more, the question or the sudden sting of antiseptic. He swore, ripely, then clenched his teeth. "Sorry."

"I've heard the word before. Was that your answer?"

"Mrs. Fletcher."

"Cilla." She leaned in close, then smiled into his eyes. Good eyes, she thought. Steady, clear. "I've embarrassed you. I didn't expect to. Almost done here. Hold this ice on it a minute."

She slid onto the bench across from him, crossed her arms on the table. By her calculations, she had two minutes tops before someone burst in the door and interrupted. "Boyd didn't think you would come today. I did. Allison is relentless when she's set her mind on something."

"Tell me about it."

"I don't know your mind, Jonah. But I know something about you, and I know what I see. So I want to tell you something."

"I didn't intend to stay this long—"

"Hush," she said mildly. "A lifetime ago. Nearly your lifetime ago, I met this cop. This irritating, fascinating, hardheaded cop. I didn't want to be interested, I certainly didn't want to be involved. My mother was a cop, and she died in the line of duty. I've never gotten over it. Not really."

She had to take a breath to steady herself, because it was perfectly true. "The last thing I wanted, the last thing I figured was good for me, was to find myself tangled up with a cop. I know how they think, what they are, what they risk. God, I didn't want that in my life. And here I am, a lifetime later. The wife of one, the mother of one."

She glanced out the window, caught sight of her husband, then her daughter. "Strange, isn't it, the way things turn out? It isn't easy, but I wouldn't give up a moment of it. Not one moment."

She patted the hand he'd laid on the table, then rose. "I'm glad you came today."

"Why?"

"Because it gave me a chance to see you and Ally together. It gave me a chance to look at you, close. An opportunity you haven't given me more than twice in, what is it, Jonah, seventeen years? And I like what I see."

Leaving him speechless, she turned to the fridge and pulled out a platter of burger patties. "Would you mind taking these to Boyd? If we don't feed the kids every couple of hours, it gets ugly."

"All right." He took the platter, struggled with himself while she just smiled at him out of the eyes Ally had inherited. "She's a lot like you, too."

"She inherited all of my and Boyd's most annoying qualities. Funny how that works." She rose on her toes, gently touched her lips to the wound at the corner of his mouth. "That comes with the treatment."

"Thanks." He shifted the tray, searched for something to say. No one in his life had ever kissed him where it hurt. "I have to get back to the city. Thank you for everything."

"You're welcome. You're welcome anytime, Jonah."

She smiled to herself as he went out. "Your turn at the plate, Boyd," she murmured. "Make it count."

Chapter 11

"It's all in the wrist," Boyd claimed, flipping a burger.

"I thought you said it was all in the timing." Ally stood, thumbs tucked into her pockets while her brother Bryant looked on, his elbow comfortably hooked on her shoulder.

"Timing is, of course, essential. There are many, many subtle aspects to the art of the barbecue."

"But when do we eat?" Bryant demanded.

"Two minutes if you're going for a burger. Another ten if you're holding out for steak." He peered through the billowing smoke as Jonah cut across the yard with a platter. "Looks like we have more supplies on the way."

"How about a burger, then steak?"

"You're tenth in line, I believe, for burger requests, son. Take a number." Boyd flipped another, sent it sizzling, then furrowed his brow as he caught sight of his wife on the side deck.

Dancing in place, she waved her arms, pointed at Jonah, pointed at Boyd, circled her fingers. He got the drift, and though he winced inwardly, gave a subtle shrug of acknowledgment.

Okay, okay, I'll talk to him. Damn it.

Cilla only smiled, then wagged her finger back and forth.

And I won't hurt him. Sheesh.

"Just set down the fresh rations, Jonah." Boyd jerked a thumb toward the high table beside the pit. "How's the lip?"

"I'll live." Jonah sent Ally a steely stare. "Especially since despite unsportsmanlike conduct by the opposing guard, I made the basket. And won."

"Lucky shot. We'll have a rematch after we eat."

"She loses," Bryant commented, "she demands a rematch. She wins, she rubs it in your face for days."

"And your point would be?" Ally fluttered her lashes at him.

"Mom would never let me hit her, because she was a girl." Bryant gave Ally's ear one hard tug. "I've always found that grossly unfair."

"Big deal. You just beat up on Keenan."

"Yeah." Instantly Bryant's face brightened. "Those were the days. I'm planning on punching on him later, for old times' sake."

"Can I watch? Like I used to."

"Naturally."

"Please. Your mother and I like to maintain the illusion we raised three well-balanced, competent adults. Don't shatter our dreams. Jonah, you haven't seen my workshop, have you?" At his daughter's answering snort, Boyd winged an eyebrow at her. "No comments. Bryant, this is a moment."

"Is it?"

"A monumental moment. I am passing the sacred tongs and spatula to you."

"Wait a minute, wait a minute." Ally elbowed her brother aside. "Why can't I do it?"

"Ah." Boyd held a hand to his heart. "How many times have I heard you say those very words in our long and exciting life together?"

Amused and fascinated by the family dynamics, Jonah watched mutiny settle over Ally's face. "Well, why can't I?"

"Allison, my treasure, there are some things a man must pass to his son. Son." Boyd laid a hand on Bryant's shoulder. "I'm trusting you with the Fletcher reputation. Don't let me down."

"Dad." Bryant wiped an imaginary tear from his eye. "I'm overwhelmed. Honored. I swear to uphold the family name, no matter what the cost."

"Take these." Boyd held out the barbecue tools. "Today, you are a man."

"That bites," Ally muttered as Boyd swung an arm around Jonah's shoulder.

"You're just a girl." Bryant leered and rubbed the tools together. "Live with it."

"She'll make him pay for that," Boyd murmured. "So, how are things?"

"Well enough." How the hell was Jonah supposed to make a quiet escape when someone or other was always dragging him somewhere? "I appreciate the hospitality today. I'm going to have to get back to the club."

"A business like that doesn't give you a lot of free time, especially in the early years." Still he steered Jonah toward a wooden structure in the far corner of the yard. "Know anything about power tools?"

"They make a great deal of noise."

Boyd gave a hoot of laughter and opened the door of the workshop. "What do you think?"

The garage-size room was full of tables, machines, shelves, tools, stacks of wood. There appeared to be a number of projects in progress, but Jonah couldn't tell what they were, or what they were intended to be.

"Impressive," he decided, diplomatically. "What do you do here?"

"I make a great deal of noise. Other than that, I haven't figured it out. I helped Keenan build a birdhouse about ten years ago. Came out pretty good. Cilla started buying me tools. Boy toys, she calls them."

He ran his hand over the guard of a skill saw. "Then I needed a place to keep them. Before I knew it, I had a fully equipped workshop. I think it was all a ploy to get me out of her hair."

"Pretty clever."

"That she is." They stood for a moment, hands in pockets, soberly studying the tools. "Okay, let's get this over with so we can both relax and get something to eat. What's going on with you and my daughter?"

Jonah couldn't say it was unexpected, but it still made his stomach clench. "We're seeing each other."

With a nod, Boyd walked over to a small square refrigerator and took out two beers. He twisted off the tops, held one out to Jonah. "And?"

Jonah tipped back the beer, then gave Boyd a level look. "What do you want me to say?"

"The truth. Though I realize what you'd like to say is that it's none of my business."

"Of course it's your business. She's your daughter."

"There we have no argument." Deciding to get comfortable, Boyd boosted himself up on a worktable. "There's a matter of intent, Jonah. I'm asking what you intend in regard to my daughter."

"I don't have any intentions. I should never have touched her. I know that."

"Really." Intrigued, Boyd cocked his head. "Mind explaining that?"

"What do you want from me? Damn it." Giving into frustration, Jonah dragged a hand through his hair.

"The first time you asked me that, in almost that same tone, you were thirteen. Your lip was bleeding then, too."

Jonah steadied himself. "I remember."

"I've never known you to forget anything, which means you'll remember what I said to you then, but I'll say it again. What do you want from *you*, Jonah?"

"I've got what I want. A decent life run in a way I can respect and enjoy. And I know why I have it. I know what I owe you, Fletch. Everything. Everything I've got, everything I am started with you. You opened doors for me, you took me on when you had no reason to."

"Whoa." Genuinely shocked, Boyd held up a hand. "Hold on."

"You changed my life. You gave me a life. I know where I'd be if it wasn't for you. I had no right to take advantage of that."

"You're sure putting a lot on me here," Boyd said quietly. "What I did, Jonah, was see a street kid with potential. And I hassled him."

Emotion swirled into Jonah's eyes. "You made me."

"Oh, Jonah, no, I didn't. You made yourself. Though God knows I'm proud to have played a part in it."

Boyd slid off the table, wandered the shop. Whatever he'd expected from this talk, it hadn't been to have his emotions stirred. To feel very much like a father being given a precious gift by a son.

"If you feel there's a debt, then pay it off now by being straight with me." He turned back. "Are you involved with Ally because she's mine?"

"In spite of it," Jonah corrected. "I stopped thinking about her being yours. If I hadn't, I wouldn't be involved with her."

It was the answer he wanted, so Boyd nodded. The boy's suffering, he thought, and couldn't find it in himself to be overly sorry about it. "Define involved."

"For God's sake, Fletch." Jonah took a long gulp of beer.

"I don't mean that area." Boyd spoke quickly, took a deep drink himself. "Let's just leave that particular area behind a firmly locked door so we don't have to punch each other."

"Fine. Good."

"I meant, what are your feelings for her?"

"I care about her."

Boyd waited a beat, nodded again. "Okay."

Jonah swore. Boyd had asked him to play straight, and he was circling. "I'm in love with her. Damn it." He closed his eyes, imagined flinging the bottle against the wall, shattering glass. It didn't help. "I'm sorry." Jonah opened his eyes again, got a slippery grip on control. "But that's as straight as it gets."

"Yeah, I'd say so."

"You know what I'm built on. You can't think I'm good enough for her."

"Of course you're not," Boyd said simply, and noticed those clear green eyes didn't so much as flicker. "She's my little girl, Jonah. No one's good enough for her. But knowing what you're built on, I'd say you're pretty close. I wonder why that surprises you. The one area I don't recall you ever being low in is esteem."

"I'm over my head here," Jonah murmured. "It's been a long time since I've been over my head in anything."

"Women do that to you. The right woman, you never really surface again. She's beautiful, isn't she?"

"Yes. She blinds me."

"She's also smart, and she's strong, and she knows how to deal with what's dished out."

Absently, Jonah rubbed his thumb over his sore lip. "No argument."

"Then my advice to you is to play it straight

with her, too. She won't let you get away with less, not for long."

"She isn't looking for anything else from me."

"You keep thinking that, son." At ease again, Boyd crossed to Jonah, laid a hand on his shoulder. "There's just one thing," he said as they started toward the door. "If you hurt her, I'll take you out. They'll never find your body."

"Well, I feel better now."

"Good. So, how do you like your steak?"

Ally saw them come out of the workshop and relaxed for the first time since the moment she'd watched them go in. Her father had his arm swung companionably around Jonah's shoulder. It looked as if they'd done no more than share a friendly beer and grunt over the power tools.

If her father had done any poking or prying into her relationship with Jonah, at least he hadn't drilled any embarrassing holes.

She liked seeing them together, liked very much witnessing the very real bond of affection and mutual respect. Her family was paramount in her life, and though she would have given her heart where her heart yearned, it would never have settled with full happiness on a man her family couldn't love.

She bobbled the bowl of potato salad, would have dropped it if Cilla hadn't made the grab.

"Butter fingers," Cilla said and set the bowl on the deck table.

"Mom."

"Hmm? We're going to run out of ice again."

"I'm in love with Jonah."

"I know, baby. Who's not blocked in? I need somebody to get some ice."

"How can you know?" Ally grabbed her mother's wrist before Cilla could go to the deck rail and shout for an ice run. "I just figured it out this second."

"Because I know you, and I see the way you are with him." Gently, she smoothed a hand over Ally's hair. "Scared or happy?"

"Both."

"Good." Cilla turned, sighed once, then kissed Ally on each cheek. "That's perfect." She slipped an arm around Ally's waist, turned to the rail. "I like him."

"Me, too. I really like who he is."

Cilla tipped her head toward her daughter's. "It's nice, isn't it, having the family together like this."

"It's wonderful. Jonah and I had a fight about coming here today."

"Looks like you won."

"Yeah. We're going to have another fight when I tell him we're getting married."

"You're your father's daughter. My money's on you."

"Place your bets," Ally suggested, and walked down the steps, crossed the lawn. It was a calculated move. She didn't mind being calculating, not when she had a point to make.

She strolled up to her father and Jonah, cupped Jonah's face in her hands and pressed her lips hard to his. He hissed, reminding her about his sore mouth. But she just laughed, shook back her hair.

"Suck it in, tough guy," she suggested and kissed him again.

His hands came to her waist, fused there, drawing her up on her toes that intimate inch.

"Dad?" She eased back down. "Mom needs more ice."

"She's just saying that to make me look bad." Boyd scanned the yard, homed in on his target. "Keenan! Go get your mother more ice."

"So…" As her father chased down her brother, Ally linked her hands at the back of Jonah's neck. "What were you talking about with my father?"

"Man stuff. What are you doing?" he demanded as she brushed her lips over his again.

"If you have to ask, I must not be doing it right."

"I'm outnumbered here, Allison. Are you trying to coax your family into stomping me into dust?"

"Don't worry. We're very big on kissing in my family."

"I noticed. Still." He drew her back.

"You've got this quietly proper streak. It's really cute. Are you having a good time?"

"Except for a couple of minor incidents," he said, deliberately tapping his finger on the corner of his mouth. "You have a nice family."

"They're great. You forget sometimes how steadying, how comforting it is to have them.

How much you depend on them for a hundred little things. My cousins will remember coming out here when they were kids, or all of us piling into that gorgeous gothic fortress of Uncle Gage's, or trooping up to the mountains to…"

"What?"

"Wait. Give me a minute." She had his hand and squeezed it as she shut her eyes and let the pieces of the puzzle tumble together. "You're drawn back," she murmured. "You're always drawn back to memories, and places where you were happy with the people who mean the most. That's why people are always going back to visit their hometown, or driving by the house where they grew up." She paused and opened her eyes as a new thought hit her. "Where did he grow up?"

She tapped a fist against Jonah's chest. "Where did he and his sister grow up? Where did they live together? Where was he happy? He has to go somewhere, has to find a place to hide, to plan. He's gone home."

She spun around and raced for the house.

She was already dialing the kitchen phone when Jonah caught up with her. "What are you doing?"

"My job. Stupid, stupid, not to think of it before! Carmichael? It's Fletcher. I need you to do a check for me. I need an address—Matthew Lyle's old address, addresses maybe. Going back to when he was a kid. There's ah…"

She paused, forced it into focus. "He was born in Iowa, and they moved around some. I can't remember when he came to Denver. The parents are dead. Yeah, you can reach me at this number." She recited it. "Or my cell phone. Thanks."

"You think he's gone back home?"

"He needs to feel close to his sister to feel safe, to feel powerful." Allison paced the kitchen as she tried to remember details of the file. "The psych profile tags him as dependent on her, even as he sees himself as her protector. She's his only real consistency, the only constant in his life. Parents divorced, kids got bounced around. Mother remarried, bounced around some more. Stepfather was…damn."

She pressed her fingers to her temple as if to push out the memory. "Ex-Marine. Very gung ho, and apparently very tough on the pudgy nerd and his devoted sister. Part of the whole authority complex comes from this instability of family life, ineffective father, the passive mother, the stern stepfather. Rocky foundations," she said as she paced.

"Lyle was bright, high IQ, but he was emotionally and socially inept. Except with his sister. His biggest trouble with the law was right after she got married. He got sloppy, careless. He was angry."

She checked her watch, urging Carmichael to hurry. "She stood by him, and it appears whatever rift there might have been between them was healed."

She leaped on the phone when it rang. "Fletcher. Yeah, what have you got?" She snatched up a pencil, began to scribble on the pad by the phone. "No, nothing out of state. He needs to stay close. Hold on." She covered the mouthpiece with her hand. "Do me a favor, Blackhawk. Would you tell my father I need to talk to him for a minute?"

It took more than a minute. She moved into her father's office, booted up his computer. With him beside her, and Carmichael on the phone, they worked through the files, picked through Matthew Lyle's history.

"See, ten years ago he was listing a P.O. Box as his address. He kept that listing for six years, even though he had a house on the lake. Bought that house nine years ago, the same year his sister married Fricks. But he held onto the P.O. Box."

"And his sister lists the same P.O. Box as her address through the same period."

"But where did they live? I'm going to go in and pin Fricks down on this one." Then she pursed her lips, considered. "Carmichael, you up for another run? See what you can find me on property in the Denver metro area listed under the names Madeline Lyle or Madeline Matthews. Run Matthew and Lyle Madeline, too."

"Good move," Boyd approved. "Good thinking."

"He likes to own things," Ally noted. "Possessions are very important to him. If he stuck in the same spot for six years, more or less, he'd want his own place—or one for his sister."

She straightened in the chair. "Did you just say bingo? Carmichael, I think I love you. Yeah, yeah. All right. I've got it. I'll let you know. Really. Thanks."

She hung up, jumped out of the chair. "Lyle Madeline owns a condo in the center of downtown."

"Good work, Detective. Contact your lieutenant and assemble your team. And Ally," Boyd added, "I want in."

"Commissioner, I'm sure we can make room for you."

It ran like clockwork. Within two hours the building was surrounded, the stairways and exits blocked. Using hand signals a dozen cops wearing Kevlar vests ranged the hallway outside of Matthew Lyle's two-level condo.

Ally had the floor plan in her head, every inch of the blueprint she'd studied. She gave the nod, and the two officers beside her hit the door with the battering ram.

She went in first, went in low.

A stream of men rushed by her and up the stairs to her right. Others fanned out to the rooms at her left. It took less than ten minutes to determine the condo was empty.

"He's been staying here." Ally gestured to

the dishes in the sink. She dipped a finger into the dirt of an ornamental lemon tree potted by the kitchen window. "Damp. He's tending house. He'll be back."

In a bedroom upstairs they found three handguns, an assault rifle and a case of ammunition. "Be prepared," Ally murmured. "I see extra clips for a nine millimeter, but I don't see the nine millimeter, so he's armed."

"Detective Fletcher?" One of her team backed out of the closet, holding a long bladed knife with gloved fingers. "Looks like our murder weapon."

"Bag it." She picked up a black-and-silver matchbook from the dresser. "Blackhawk's." She shifted her eyes to her father. "That's his target. The only question is when."

Night had fallen when Ally confronted Jonah in his office. The man was mule stubborn, she thought. And more, he was just plain wrong.

"You close down for twenty-four hours. Forty-eight tops."

"No."

"I can close you down."

"No, you can't. And if you wrangle it, it'll take you longer than the forty-eight hours, which makes the entire process moot."

She dropped into a chair. It was important to stay calm, she reminded herself. Vital to stay in control. She hissed out a breath, then a stream of violent and inventive oaths.

"I don't believe your last suggestion is possible, regardless of my strength and flexibility."

She bolted forward. "Listen to me."

"No, you listen to me." His voice was quiet, cool, inflexible. "I could do what you're asking. What's to stop him from waiting me out? I close down, he goes under. I open, he surfaces. We could play that game indefinitely. I prefer running my own game, on my own turf."

"I'm not going to say you don't have a point, because you do. But we'll nail him within two days. I promise you. All you have to do is shut the place down, take a little vacation. My parents have a great place in the mountains."

"Would you be coming with me?"

"Of course not. I have to stay here and close this thing."

"You stay. I stay."

"You're a civilian."

"Exactly, and until this is a police state, I have a right to run my business and come and go as I please."

She wanted to tear at her hair, but knew that would just amuse him. "It's my job to keep you alive to run your business."

He got to his feet. "Is that what you think? Are you my shield, Ally? Is that why you've been wearing your gun until we're up here behind locked doors? Is that why you keep it within reach even when we are here?"

He came around the desk, even as she cursed herself for the slip. "I don't like the implications of that."

She met him toe to toe. "You're a target."

"So are you."

"This is a waste of time."

He spun her around before she could stalk to the elevator. "You will not stand in front of me." He said it slowly, distinctly, with that rare glint of ready temper in his eyes. "Understand that."

"Don't tell me how to do my job."

"Don't tell me how to live my life."

She threw her head back, released a muffled scream. "All right. Okay. forget it. We do it the hard way. Here's the deal. Twenty-four-hour guards outside. Cops in soft clothes in the bar and club areas at all times. You take on undercover officers as kitchen and wait help."

"I don't like that deal."

"Tough. Take it or leave it. Leave it and I pull strings and have you slapped into protective custody so fast even a slick customer like you won't be able to slide through the knots. I can do it, Blackhawk, and I will. My father will help me do it, because he cares about you. Please." She grabbed him by the lapels. "Do it for me."

"Forty-eight hours," he agreed. "And in the meantime, I put out word on the street I'm looking for him."

"Don't—"

"That's the deal. It's fair."

"All right. That's the deal."

"Now, what would you like to bet that I can go downstairs right now and pick out every cop you've already planted?"

She puffed out her cheeks, then showed her teeth in a smile. "No bet. I don't suppose I can convince you to stay up here tonight?"

He traced a fingertip down the center of her body. "I will if you will."

"That's what I figured." Sometimes compromise, however annoying, was the only out. "Hold that thought until closing."

"That I have no problem with." He walked over to call for the elevator. "Tonight, or tomorrow night."

"Yeah. It's just as likely, more really, that they'll take him at the condo. But if he slips through the net, or senses anything, it'll be here. And it'll be soon."

"Will's got good eyes. He'll know what to look for."

"I don't want you, or any of your people taking chances. If he's spotted, you tell me." She glanced over, caught him studying her. "What?"

"Nothing." But he traced his fingers over her

cheek. "When you've closed this down, can you take any time?"

"What do you mean time?"

"A few days. Away. Somewhere away."

"I might be talked into that. Do you have anywhere in mind?"

"No. Pick it."

"Well, aren't you open-minded and daring? I'll start thinking." She took a step out of the elevator, already shifting her focus, but he took her arm.

"Ally?"

"Yeah."

There was too much to say. Entirely too much to feel. And it wasn't the time, not the time to play it straight or any other way. "Later. We'll get into it later."

Chapter 12

Traditionally business at Blackhawk's was light on Sunday nights. There was no live music as a lure, and the first day of the work week loomed heavily.

Ally decided a great many people in Denver were taking advantage of the gorgeous weather and mild evening, and most who strolled in out of the night lingered an hour or more over their drinks or bowls of guacamole and chips.

She watched the entrance, checked the exits,

studied faces and counted heads. Throughout the evening she slipped into the lounge at regular intervals to check in with the stakeout at Lyle's condo.

An hour before closing, and still he hadn't been spotted.

Itchy, she roamed the floor, checking faces, watching doors. The crowd was thinning out, and she imagined there'd be no more than a scatter of customers left by last call.

Where was he? she asked herself. Where the hell was he? He'd run out of places to hide.

"Detective." Jonah danced his fingers over her shoulder. "I thought you'd be interested to know one of my sources reports a man fitting Lyle's description has been asking questions about me."

"When?" She gripped his arm and pulled him toward the alcove. "Where?"

"Tonight, actually. At my other place."

"Fast Break?" She swore, whipped out her phone. "We didn't put anyone there. They never hit there. It's not his style."

"I'd say that holds true." He laid a hand over hers before she could dial the phone. "The bartender there just got in touch. Apparently Lyle—I assume it was Lyle though he was wearing glasses and sporting a beard—dropped into Fast Break a few hours ago, loitered at the bar, started asking if I ever came in."

"Hold on." Ally tapped his hand away and put her call through. "Balou? Cut a pair of uniforms loose from the condo. Tell them to see the bartender at Fast Break. The address is…"

She looked at Jonah, repeated the address he gave her. "Lyle was in there tonight. He's reported to be wearing a beard and glasses. Make sure that gets out."

She disconnected, looked back at Jonah.

"As I was saying," he continued, "my man didn't think anything of it initially, then it started to bother him. He says Lyle was jumpy. Hung around about a half hour then said to tell me he'd see me around."

"His center's crumbling. He's psyching himself up to move." She wanted Jonah out of the way. "Look, why don't you go up, give your man another call. Let him know a couple of cops are on their way."

"Do I look like I'd fall for that lame a con?"

He strolled away from her to check on a table of customers who were preparing to leave.

The shouts came from the kitchen, followed by an explosive crash of dishes. Ally had her gun out, bolting for the door when it burst open.

He'd ditched the glasses, and the beard was a thin and scraggly dusting over his chin. But she saw she'd been right. He'd psyched himself up. His eyes were wide and wild.

And he had the barrel of the nine millimeter pressed to the soft underside of Beth's jaw.

"Don't move! Don't anybody move!" he shouted over the screams, the rush of running feet as customers scattered.

"Stay calm. Everybody stay calm." She side-stepped, kept her gun trained on him, her eyes trained on him. Forced herself to block out Beth's terrified face. "Lyle, take it easy. You want to let her go."

"I'll kill her. I'll blow her head off."

"You do that, I kill you. Think, you need to think. Where does that get you?"

"Put your gun down. Drop it, kick it over here, or she's dead."

"I'm not going to do that. And neither are any of the other cops in here. You know how many weapons you have aimed at you right now, Lyle? Look around. Do a count. It's over. Save yourself."

"I'll kill her." His gaze jittered around the room, bounced off guns. "Then I'll kill you. That'll be enough."

Someone was sobbing. Out of the corner of her eye she could see the bar area where civilians were being rushed outside to safety.

"You want to live, don't you? Madeline would want you to live."

"Don't you say her name! Don't you say my sister's name!" He shoved the gun harder against Beth's throat and made her cry out.

No place to run, Ally thought. His sister had had no place to run, and still she'd turned and fired.

"She loved you." Ally edged closer, keeping his focus on her. If she could get him to lower the gun, a few inches, get him to shift it toward her. Away from Beth. "She died for you."

"She was all I had! I got nothing to lose now. I want the cop who killed her, and I want Black-hawk. Now! Right now or she dies!"

Out of the corner of her eye, Ally saw Jonah move forward. "Look at me!" She shouted the words. "I'm the one who killed your sister."

He screamed, one long howl as he jerked the gun away from Beth, swung it toward Ally. There was a burst of gunfire, a blur of movement, wails of terror.

With fear locked in her throat, Ally rushed forward to where Jonah lay tangled with Lyle. Blood coated them both.

"Damn you! Damn, are you crazy?" With urgent hands she began to pat him down, looking for wounds. He'd thrown himself at the gun. In front of the gun.

He was breathing. She held onto that. He was breathing, and she would make sure he kept on breathing. "Jonah. Oh God."

"I'm all right. Stop poking at me."

"All right? You jumped into crossfire. You nearly got yourself killed."

"You, too." He looked past her to where the

starry floor was cracked an inch from where she'd stood.

"I'm wearing a vest."

"And that takes care of your hard head, too?" He sat back as a cop turned Lyle over.

"He's gone."

Jonah spared Lyle's face one glance, then looked into Ally's eyes. "I'd like to calm my customers down."

"You're not calming anyone down." Ally rose with him. "You've got blood all over you. Is all of it his?"

"Mostly."

"What do you mean mostly?"

"I'm going to deal with my customers and my people." He held her at arm's length before she could snatch at him again. "Do your job, and let me do mine."

He turned away to take Beth from the female officer who was holding her. "Come on, Beth, come on with me. Everything's all right now."

Ally pressed her fingers to her eyes then looked down at what was left of Matthew Lyle. "Yeah, everything's dandy."

* * *

"Slipped in the back," Hickman told her while they sat in the nearly empty club. The civilians were gone, the body had been removed and the crime scene unit was packing up.

She wondered idly what time it was, and how soon she could fall on her face and tune the world out. "He stopped being smart," she said. "He stopped thinking."

"You got that right," Hickman agreed. "Got himself one of those white kitchen uniforms, slapped on a wig and glasses. Before the cop who spotted him could call in or move, all hell broke loose."

"He didn't think we were smart enough to close him in. I saw his face when he spotted all the cops. Pure shock. My guess? He figured on breaking in here, taking Jonah down, me if I was around, then he's got hostages. He'd demand we turn over the cop who killed his sister. He really figured we'd do it, and he'd get out."

"Arrogant. Speaking of which, it was pretty cocky, telling him you were the one he wanted."

"I don't know why he didn't spot me in the first place."

"You look different." Hickman scanned a look up, then down. "Very un-Fletcherlike."

"Give me a break, Hickman. I look how I look. I'll tell you how it was. He came in here for Jonah. When he looked at me, all he saw was cop—no face, no form, just another cop. He didn't put me together with the one who'd worked here."

"Maybe." He got to his feet. "I guess we'll never know."

He glanced over at the starburst crack in the floor. "Too bad about that—classy floor. Bet it'll cost an arm and two legs to fix it."

"Maybe he'll leave it like that. Conversation piece. Draw a crowd."

"Yeah." The idea tickled Hickman. "We'd've taken him out right away, you know, but he would've gotten that shot off anyway. At that range, the vest would've stopped the bullet. Probably. But one way or the other, if the shot hadn't been deflected, you'd have been seriously hurt."

Absently she rubbed a hand between her breasts, imagined the breathless pain. "You ever taken one in the vest?"

"Nope, but Deloy did. Had himself a softball-size bruise." Hickman held up his hands, made a circle. "Knocked him clean off his feet, too, and tossed him back like a rag doll. Ended up with a concussion where his head hit the pavement. That has to hurt."

"I'll take it over a bullet."

"Any day of the week. I'm going home." He got to his feet. "See you tomorrow."

"Yeah. Nice work."

"Back at you. Oh, your guy's in the kitchen, getting patched up."

"What do you mean patched up?"

"Caught a little friendly fire. Just a nick."

"He's shot? *Shot?* Why didn't anyone tell me?"

Hickman didn't bother to answer. She was already gone.

Ally slammed into the kitchen, her eyes dark and furious when she saw Jonah at one of the worktables, stripped to the waist, calmly drinking a brandy while Will rolled gauze over his upper arm.

"Hold it. Just hold it. Let me see that." She slapped Will away, unwound the gauze and poked at the long shallow cut until Jonah pushed her face up with the heel of his hand on her chin.

"Ouch," he said.

"Put that drink down, you're going to the hospital."

He kept his eyes on hers, lifted the brandy. Sipped. "No."

"No, my butt. What is this? Some idiot, male, macho deal? You've been shot."

"Not really. Grazed is more the accepted term. Now if you don't mind, Will's got a kinder touch with this than you. I'd like him to finish so he can go home."

"It could get infected."

"I could get hit by a truck, but I don't intend for either to happen."

"It's okay, Ally, really." Playing peacemaker, Will patted her shoulder before picking up the gauze again. "I cleaned it real good. We got some worse in the old days, didn't we, Jonah?"

"Sure did. Looks like I'm another scar up on you now."

"Well, isn't that nice?" Ally grabbed the brandy, glugged.

"I thought you hated brandy."

"I do."

"Why don't you get a glass of wine," Will suggested. "I'm nearly done here."

"I'm fine. I'm okay." Ally blew out a breath. Now, she thought, after everything, her hands wanted to shake. "Damn it, Blackhawk. I was probably the one who shot you."

"Probably. I've decided to weigh in the circumstances and not hold it against you."

"That's real big of you. Now listen to me—"

"Frannie went home with Beth," he added, wanting to distract her. "She's okay. Shaky yet, but okay. She wanted to thank you, but you were busy."

"There we go." Will stepped back. "Your arm's in a lot better shape than your shirt. I'd say that's a loss." He held up the bloodstained linen and made Ally's stomach turn over. "Want me to go up and get you a fresh one before I go?"

"No. Thanks." Jonah lifted his arm, flexed. "Nice job. Haven't lost your touch."

"All in a day's work." Will picked up his discarded jacket. "You sure stand up, Ally.

Could've been an awful mess out there tonight.
But you sure stand up."

"All in a day's work."

"I'll lock up. 'Night."

Ally sat at the table, waited until she heard
silence. "Okay, smart guy, what the hell were
you thinking? You interfered with a police operation."

"Oh, I don't know. Maybe I was thinking that
lunatic was going to kill you. It bothered me."
He held out the brandy snifter. "How about a
refill, since you drank mine."

"Fine. Sit here and swill brandy and look
stoic." She shoved back, grabbed the glass, then
gave in and wrapped her arms around his neck.
"Don't *ever* scare me like that again."

"I won't if you won't. No, just stay right there
a minute." He turned his face into her hair,
breathed deep. "I'm going to see you stepping
in front of that gun for a long time. That's hard."

"I know. I know it is."

"I'll deal with that, Ally, because that's the
way it is." He drew her back, his eyes intense
on hers. "There are some things you need to

figure out if you can deal with. If you want to deal with."

"What are they?"

He rose to get the brandy himself, poured, set the bottle on the table. "Are there still cops in my place?"

"Other than me?"

"Yeah, other than you."

"No. We're clear."

"Then sit down."

"Sounds very serious." She pulled up her chair. "I'm sitting."

"My mother left when I was sixteen." He didn't know why he started there. It just seemed to be the spot. "I couldn't blame her, still don't. My father was a hard man, and she was tired of it."

"She left you with him?"

"I was self-sufficient."

"You were sixteen."

"Ally. I was never sixteen the way you were. And I had your father."

Everything inside her softened. "That's a lovely thing to say."

"It's just fact. He made me go to school. He came down on me when I needed it, which was most of the time. And he was the first person in my life to ever tell me I was worth anything. To ever see I might be. He's…I don't know anyone who comes up to him."

She reached across the table, took his hand. "I love him, too."

"Let me get through some of this." He squeezed her hand, then drew his away. "I didn't go to college, even Fletch couldn't browbeat me into that. I took some business courses because it suited me. When I was twenty, my father died. Three packs of cigarettes a day and a general meanness catches up with you. It was long and ugly, and when it was over, the only thing I felt was relief."

"Is that supposed to make me think less of you?"

"There's a contrast here, and you see it as well as I do."

"Yeah, you had a lousy childhood. I had a great one. As fate would have it, we both got lucky and ended up with Boyd Fletcher as a father. Don't look at me like that. That's exactly what he is to you."

"I'm going to make something clear to you before this goes any farther. I wasn't a victim, Allison. I was a survivor, and used whatever methods worked. I stole and cheated and conned, and I don't apologize for it. Things would've turned out differently if I hadn't had your father hounding me. But they didn't."

"I think that was my point."

"Don't interrupt. I'm a businessman. I don't steal or cheat because I don't have to. That doesn't mean I don't play the game my way."

"A real tough guy aren't you? Blackhawk, you're a fraud. Cool customer, slick hands, icy stare. And this big, soft heart. Soft, hell, it's gooey."

Amused at the speechless shock on his face, she got up, sauntered to the fridge and hunted up an open bottle of white wine.

She wasn't tired anymore, she realized. She was revved.

"Do you think I didn't run you, pal? Run your friends, get the stories? You gather up your sick and wounded like a mama chick."

Enjoying herself now, Ally drew out the stopper, found a glass. "Frannie—got her off the streets, got her clean, gave her work. Will—straightened him up, paid off his debts before he got his knees capped, gave him a suit and some dignity."

"None of that's relevant."

"I'm not finished." She poured the wine. "The iceman got Beth into a woman's shelter, bought her kids presents from Santa Claus when she didn't have the money or the energy to deal with it. Jonah Blackhawk was buying Barbie dolls."

"I did not buy dolls." That was going just a little too far. "Frannie did. And it has nothing to do with this."

"Yeah, right. Then there's Maury, one of your line chefs." She sat down, wiggled into the chair and propped her feet up. "And the dough you lent him—and I use the word lent advisedly—to help his mother through a bad patch."

"Shut up."

She merely smiled, dipped a finger into her wine, licked it. "Sherry, the little busgirl, who's working her way through college. Who paid her tuition last semester when she couldn't scrape it together? Why, I believe it was you. And what about Pete the bartender's little problem last year when an uninsured driver totaled his car?"

"Investing in people is good business."

"That's your story, you stick to it."

Irritation and embarrassment warred for top gun inside him. He tossed his weight to the side of irritation. "You're ticking me off, Allison."

"*Ooooh,* really?" She leaned forward, leading with her chin. "Go ahead, hard case, slap me around and shut me up. Dare you."

"Be careful." He said it, meant it, then pushed to his feet. "This is irrelevant, and isn't getting us anywhere."

She crossed her ankles and made clucking noises.

"You're really asking for it."

"Yeah, yeah. I'm shaking. Sucker."

He cracked and lifted her right off the chair. "One more word. I swear, it's only going to take one more word."

She bit him, one quick nip on his already tender mouth. "Softy."

He pushed her aside and spun toward the door.

"Where you going?"

"To put on a damn shirt. I can't talk to you."

"Then I'll just have to rip it off you again. I've got a soft spot for wounded tough guys with gooey centers." And laughing, she launched herself at him, landed piggyback. "I'm crazy about you, Blackhawk."

"Go away. Go arrest somebody. I've had enough of cops for one day."

"You'll never get enough of me." She bit his earlobe, his shoulder. "Come on, shake me off."

He would have. He told himself he could have. It was just his bad luck he looked down and saw the scar in the floor. From a bullet meant for her.

He dragged her around, yanked her against him so hard, so fast, she swore her ribs knocked together. His mouth was on hers, fused there with a heat borne of desperation.

"Better. Much better. Here, Jonah. Now. We both need to make it right again. I need you to love me. Like our lives depended on it."

He was on the floor with her, without any thought but to prove to himself that she was whole and safe and alive beneath him.

The cool, hard surface of the floor might have been a feather bed, or clouds, or the jagged, unforgiving peaks of a mountain. Nothing mattered but that she was wrapped around him, that her breath was fast and hot against his skin, that her heart beat like wild wings against his.

All the fear, the tension, the ugliness poured out of her when he touched her. Her hands tangled with his, fighting to strip away boundaries. Until they were free to drive together.

When he filled her—temper, passion, desperation—it was like coming home.

His breath was in rags, his system spent, and still he rocked against her.

"Just hold me a minute more." She pressed her face against his shoulder. "Just hold me." But she felt the warm wetness on her fingers, and pulled away. "Damn it. You're bleeding again. Let me fix it."

"It's fine. It's all right."

"It'll only take a minute."

"Ally, leave it be."

The snap of his voice had her eyes narrowing. "Don't think you can step back from me now. Don't think you'll get away with it this time."

"Just get dressed." He pushed back his hair and began to follow his own orders.

"Fine." She snatched at clothes, dragged them on. "You want to go another round, we'll go another round. You stupid son of a bitch."

He heard the tremor in her voice, cursed her. Cursed himself. "Don't cry. That's playing dirty."

"I'm not crying. You think I'd cry over you?"

He could feel his heart start to shatter as he brushed a tear off her cheek with his thumb. "Don't."

She sniffled, flicked her hands over her face to dry it and sneered. "Sucker."

Fury whipped into his eyes and scalded her. She couldn't have been more delighted. She got to her feet before he did, but it was close.

"You're in love with me." She punched her fist against his chest. "And you won't admit it. That doesn't make you tough, it makes you hardheaded."

"You weren't listening to me before."

"You weren't listening to me, either, so we're even."

"Listen now." He grabbed her face with both hands. "You have connections."

"Why, you insulting…" She wondered why the top of her head didn't fly off. "How dare you talk about my family's money at a time like this."

"I don't mean money." He jerked her up to her toes, then dropped her back on the flat of her feet again. "Now who's stupid? Money's nothing. I don't give a damn about your portfolio. I have my own. I'm talking about emotional connections. Foundations, roots, for God's sake."

"You have your own there, too. Frannie. Will. Beth. My father." She waved a hand, settling down again. "But I get you. You're saying, basically, that someone like me, who comes from the kind of place I come from, should hook herself up with a man who say, comes from a good, upstanding family. Probably upper middle class. He should have a good education, and hold a straight job. A profession. Like say a lawyer or a doctor. Is that the theme here?"

"More or less."

"Interesting. Yes, that's interesting," she said with a considering nod. "I can see the logic in that. Hey, you know who fits that bill to a tee? Dennis Overton. Remember him? Stalker, tire slasher, general pain in the ass?"

She'd turned it around and boxed him into his own corner. All he could do was steam.

"Don't cop to excuses, Blackhawk, if you haven't got the guts to tell me how you feel about me, and what you want for us."

She flipped her hair back, tucked in her shirt. "My work is done here. See you around, pal."

He got to the door before she did. He was good at that. But this time he slapped a hand on it, held it closed while she glared at him. "You don't walk until we're finished."

"I said I was finished." She jerked on the door.

"I'm not. Shut up and listen."

"You tell me to shut up one more time, and—"

He shut her up. One hard, exasperated kiss. "I've never loved another woman. Never even came close. So cut me a damn break here."

Her heart did a lovely bounding leap. But she nodded, stepped back. "Okay. Spill it."

"You hit me between the eyes the first minute you walked in the room. I still can't see straight."

"Well." She backed up, slid onto a stool. "I'm liking this so far. Keep going."

"You see that? That right there." He stabbed a finger at her. "Anyone else would want to deck you."

"But not you. You love that about me."

"Apparently." He crossed to her, laid his hands on the bar on either side of her. "I love you, so that's it."

"Oh, I don't think so. Make me a deal."

"You want a deal? Here it is. You ditch the apartment and move in, officially, upstairs."

"Full gym and sauna privileges?"

Half the knots in his stomach loosened when he laughed. "Yeah."

"So far, I can live with it. What else are you offering me?"

"Nobody's ever going to love you like I do. I guarantee it. And nobody's ever going to put up with you. But I will."

"Same goes. But that's not enough."

Those wonderful eyes narrowed on her face. "What do you want?"

She rested her back against the bar. "Marriage."

Now those narrowed eyes darkened. "Do you mean that?"

"I say what I mean. Now I could ask you, but I have to figure that a guy who makes a habit of opening doors for women, and buying Christmas presents for little children—"

"Leave that part alone."

"Okay." But she sat up, brushed her knuckles over his cheek. "We'll just say I figure you've got enough of a traditional guy streak to want to propose on your own. So, I'll let you." She linked her hands at the back of his neck. "I'm waiting."

"I'm just thinking. It's the middle of the night. We're in a bar and my arm's bleeding."

"So's your mouth."

"Yeah." He swiped at it with the back of his hand. "I guess that makes it close to perfect for you and me."

"Works for me. Jonah. You work for me."

He pulled the clip out of her hair, tossed it aside. "First tell me you love me. Use my name."

"I love you, Jonah."

"Then marry me, and let's see where it takes us."

"That's a deal."

Epilogue

With a howl of outrage, Ally bolted up from the sofa. "Off side! Off side! What, are those refs blind? Did you see that?" Instead of kicking in the TV, which occurred to her, she settled for leaning down and pounding on Jonah's shoulder.

"You're just mad because your team's losing, and you're going to owe me."

"I don't know what you're talking about." She sniffed, pushing back her hair. "My team is *not* going to lose, despite corrupt and myopic officials." But it looked very dim for her side. She planted her hands on her hips. "Besides, must I remind you there is no bet because you don't have a license for gambling."

He skimmed his eyes down her long black robe. "You're not wearing your badge."

"Metaphorically, Blackhawk." She leaned over to kiss him. "I'm always wearing my badge." Then she narrowed her eyes. "You swear you didn't hear who won this game? You have no information?"

"Absolutely not."

But she didn't like the way he smiled at her. They'd missed the regular Monday night broadcast and were watching the hotly contested football game on videotape. "I don't know about you. You're slippery."

"We made a deal." He skimmed his hand up the sleeve of her robe, trailing his fingers over flesh. "I never go back on a deal." He reached for the remote, paused the screen. "Since you're up..." He held up his empty glass. "How about a refill?"

"I got it last time."

"You were up last time, too. If you'd sit down and stay down, you wouldn't get tagged."

Conceding his point, she took the glass. "Don't start the game until I get back."

"Wouldn't think of it."

She headed back to the kitchen. There were times she missed the apartment on top of the club. But even a couple of die-hard urbanites needed a little elbow room, she thought. And the house suited them. So did marriage, she thought with a contented sigh as she poured Jonah's habitual bottled water over ice.

There'd been a lot of changes in the eighteen months since they, well, closed the deal, she supposed. Good changes. The kind lives were built on. They were building strong, and they were building solid.

Sipping his water, she walked back to the great room and frowned when she found it empty. Then with a shake of her head, she set the glass down. She knew just where to find him.

She wound her way quietly through the house, and stopped at the door to the bedroom.

The winter moonlight streamed through the windows, glowing over him, and the infant he held in his arms. Love burst through her, a nova of feeling, then settled again to a steady warmth.

"You woke her up."

"She was awake."

"You woke her up," Ally repeated, crossing to him. "Because you can't keep your hands off her."

"Why should I?" He pressed his lips to his daughter's head. "She's mine."

"No question of that." Ally traced a finger over the baby's soft black hair. "She's going to have your eyes."

The idea of it was a staggering thrill. He looked down at that perfect little face, with those dark and mysterious eyes of the newborn. He could see his whole life in those eyes. Sarah's eyes.

"You can't tell at two weeks. The books say it takes longer."

"She's going to have your eyes," Ally repeated. She draped an arm around his waist and together they studied their miracle. "Is she hungry?"

"No. She's just a night person." And his, like the

woman beside him was his. Two years before they hadn't existed for him. Now they were the world.

He turned his head, leaning down as Ally lifted her mouth. As the kiss sweetened, the baby stirred in his arms. He shifted, tucking Sarah's head on his shoulder with a natural grace that never failed to make Ally smile.

He'd taken to fatherhood as if he'd only been waiting for the moment. Then again, she thought, thinking of her own father, he'd had a wonderful teacher.

She angled her head, studied the two of them. "I guess she wants to watch the game now."

Jonah rubbed his cheek over his daughter's hair. "She mentioned it."

"She'll just fall asleep."

"So will you."

With a laugh, Ally took the blanket from the bassinet. "Give her up," she said, holding out her arms.

"No."

Ally rolled her eyes. "Okay, you get her till halftime, then it's my turn."

"Deal."

With the baby on his shoulder and his hand
linked with the woman's he loved, he went out
to enjoy the night.

* * * * *

Danger walks in the darkness…

*Don't miss the next great story from bestselling
author Nora Roberts!*

*Risky Business
by
Nora Roberts*

Coming next month!

**"I felt the knife against my throat and thought
I was going to die."**

*Liz Palmer runs a dive business in the quiet
tranquillity of a Caribbean island. Tranquil, that is,
until a routine trip over the reef reveals the body of
her newest employee – diver Jerry Sharpe. But when
his brother, Jonas, shows up asking questions, Liz
can't see how she can help. She barely knew Jerry.*

*Then someone breaks into Liz's apartment, intent
on her murder. Liz realises that she is already more
involved in Jonas's quest to unravel Jerry's murky
past than she wanted to be. And now Jonas and Liz
will be drawn into a dangerous criminal underworld
that could cost them both their lives…*

Read on for a preview!

RISKY BUSINESS

"Watch your step, please. Please, watch your step. Thank you." Liz took a ticket from a sunburned man with palm trees on his shirt, then waited patiently for a woman with two bulging straw baskets to dig out another one.

"I hope you haven't lost it, Mabel. I told you to let me hold it."

"I haven't lost it," the woman said testily before she pulled out the little piece of blue cardboard.

"Thank you. Please take your seats." It was several more minutes before everyone was settled and she could take her own. "Welcome aboard the *Fantasy*, ladies and gentlemen."

With her mind on a half dozen other things, Liz began her opening monologue. She gave an absentminded nod to the man on the dock who cast off the ropes before she started the engine. Her voice was pleasant and easy as she took another look at her watch. They were already fifteen minutes behind schedule. She gave one last scan of the beach, skimming by lounge chairs, over bodies already stretched and oiled slick, like offerings to the sun. She couldn't hold the tour any longer.

The boat swayed a bit as she backed it from the dock and took an eastern course. Though her thoughts were scattered, she made the turn from the coast expertly. She could have navigated the boat with her eyes closed. The air that ruffled around her face was soft and already warming, though the hour was early. Harmless and powder-puff white, clouds dotted the horizon. The water, churned by the engine, was as blue as the guidebooks promised. Even after ten years, Liz took none of it for granted – especially her liveli-hood. Part of that depended on an atmosphere that made muscles relax and problems disappear.

Behind her in the long, bullet-shaped craft were eighteen people seated on padded benches. They were already murmuring about the fish and formations they saw through the glass bottom. She doubted if any of them thought of the worries they'd left behind at home.

'Below, you see the wreck of a forty-passenger Convair airliner lying upside down." She slowed the boat so that her passengers could examine the wreck and the divers out for early explorations. Bubbles rose from air tanks like small silver disks. "The wreck's no tragedy," she continued. "It was sunk for a scene in a movie and provides divers with easy entertainment."

Her job was to do the same for her passengers, she reminded herself. It was simple enough when she had a mate on board. Alone, she had to captain the boat, keep up the light, informative banter, deal with snorkel equipment, serve lunch and count heads. It just hadn't been possible to wait any longer for Jerry.

She muttered to herself a bit as she increased speed. It wasn't so much that she minded the extra work, but she felt her paying customers were entitled to the best she could offer. She should have known better than to depend on him. She could have easily arranged for someone else to come along.

When a woman screamed behind her, Liz let off the throttle. Before she could turn, the scream was joined by another. Her first thought was that perhaps they'd seen one of the sharks that occasionally visited the reefs. Set to calm and soothe, Liz let the boat drift in the current. A woman was weeping in her husband's arms, another held her child's face protectively against her shoulder. The rest were staring down through the clear glass. Liz took off her sunglasses as she walked down the two steps into the cabin.

"Please try to stay calm. I promise you, there's nothing down there that can hurt you in here."

A man with a Nikon around his neck and an orange sun visor over a balding dome gave her a steady look.

"Miss, you'd better radio the police."

Liz looked down through the clear glass, through the crystal blue water. Her heart rose to her throat. She saw now why Jerry had stood her up. He was lying on the white sandy bottom with an anchor chain wrapped around his chest.

Passion. Power. Suspense.
It's time to fall under the spell of Nora Roberts.

From No. 1 *New York Times* bestselling author Nora Roberts

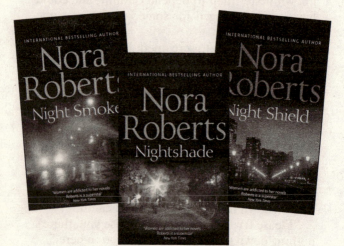

Nightshade

When a teenager gets caught up in making sadistic violent films, Colt Nightshade and Lieutenant Althea Grayson must find her before she winds up dead...

Night Smoke

When Natalie Fletcher's office is set ablaze, she must find out who wants her ruined – before someone is killed...

Night Shield

When a revengeful robber leaves blood-stained words on Detective Allison Fletcher's walls, she knows her cop's shield won't be enough to protect her...

Passion. Power. Suspense.
It's time to fall under the spell of Nora Roberts.